Cathrine Lucy Wilhelmina Cleveland

**The True Story of Kaspar Hause**

Cathrine Lucy Wilhelmina Cleveland

**The True Story of Kaspar Hause**

ISBN/EAN: 9783744662666

Printed in Europe, USA, Canada, Australia, Japan

Cover: Foto ©Raphael Reischuk / pixelio.de

More available books at **www.hansebooks.com**

# THE TRUE STORY

OF

# KASPAR HAUSER

From Official Documents

BY

## THE DUCHESS OF CLEVELAND

London

## MACMILLAN AND CO.

AND NEW YORK

1893

# KASPAR HAUSER

THE story of Kaspar Hauser is both curious and instructive. It shows on how commonplace and unpromising a foundation a myth of European celebrity may rest.

One afternoon in May 1828 (it was an Easter Monday), two men, standing talking together in the Unschlittsplatz, outside the Neue Thor (New Gate) of Nuremberg, were hailed by a country lad, who asked his way to the Neue Thor Strasse (New Gate Street). He was a fresh-complexioned boy of seventeen or there-abouts, dressed like a countryman, and decidedly short of his age ; his clothes were dusty, as from a long tramp, and he looked jaded, but he came up to them with a quick, firm step. He then pulled a letter out of his pocket addressed, with all the usual German formalities, to "the Captain of the 4th Squadron of the Schmolischer

B

Regiment, Neue Thor Strasse, Nuremberg."
One of the men, a shoemaker named Weichmann, offered to take him part of the way, as
he was himself going in that direction, and they
had a little talk together as they went. He
wanted to know whether the Neue Thor had
been only just built. He was asked where
he came from. "From Ratisbon." Had he
ever been in Nuremberg before? "No, it was
the first time." He spoke the Low Bavarian
dialect, and from his appearance Weichmann
judged him to be a groom or stable boy. As
they passed through the Neue Thor, he pulled off
his hat to the corporal on guard, again produced
his letter, and received directions where to take
it. Here Weichmann and he parted company.

When he reached the Captain's house, the
Captain was not at home. He either gave or
wrote down his name, "Kaspar Hauser," and
the groom who opened the door allowed him
to await his master's return. They sat down
together on a stone bench in the stables. The
groom remarked he looked tired and dusty, and
asked where he came from. He replied, "I
must not say," then burst into tears, and said
he had been forced to travel day and night, and
had to be carried when he could no longer walk.
The groom compassionately offered him meat

and beer, but he would touch nothing but bread
and water. When shown the horses, he fondled
and stroked them, saying, " There were five like
those where I came from." He also mentioned
that he had to cross the frontier every day in
going to school. At last, thoroughly tired out,
he coiled himself up in the straw and fell fast
asleep.

The Captain in due time came home,
opened the letter he had brought, and read as
follows :

" Honoured Sir—I send you a lad who wishes
to serve his King truly; this lad was brought to
me on October 7, 1812. I am a poor day-
labourer with ten children of my own ; I have
enough to do to get on at all. His mother
asked me to bring up the boy. I asked her no
questions, nor have I given notice to the county
police that I had taken the boy. I thought I
ought to take him as my son. I have brought
him up as a good Christian ; and since 1812 I
have never let him go a step away from the
house, so no one knows where he has been
brought up, and he himself does not know the
name of my house, nor of the place ; you may
ask him, but he can't tell you. I have taught
him to read and to write ; he can write as well

as myself.[1]　When we ask him what he would like to be, he says a soldier, like his father.　If he had parents (which he has not), he would have been a scholar; only show him a thing, and he can do it.

"I have only taken him as far as Neumarkt; from there he went on by himself.　I have told him that when he is a soldier I may come and see him, otherwise he is off my hands.

"Honoured Sir, you may question him, but he don't know where I live.　I brought him away in the middle of the night; he can't find his way back.

"I respectfully take my leave.　I don't give my name, as I might be punished.

"And he has not a single kreuzer" (the smallest German coin) "by him, for I have nothing myself.　If you won't keep him, you must knock him on the head or hang him up."

Dated, "From the Bavarian frontier; place not named."

Enclosed was another letter, written in Latin characters, but apparently with the same ink:

"The boy is baptized; his name is Kaspar;

---

[1] The handwriting of this letter was almost exactly similar to Kaspar's.

his other name you must give him. I ask you to bring him up. His father was a Schmolischer (trooper). When he is seventeen, send him to Nuremberg to the 6th Schmolische Regiment : that is where his father was. I beg you to bring him up till he is seventeen. He was born on April 30, 1812. I am a poor girl ; I can't keep the boy ; his father is dead."

The Captain then questioned the boy, who only answered, " My foster-father bade me say, I don't know, your honour " ; then pulling off his hat, he added, " He told me I was always to say your honour, and take off my hat." He repeated over and over again that he wanted to be a trooper as his father had been, but would give no further account of himself, nor tell where he came from. The Captain evidently did not fancy this mysterious and diminutive recruit. He did not like the tone of the letter, and sent him to the police-station as a runaway. From thence he was, after three hours' detention, transferred to the Castle, and lodged in a prison cell—surely a very harsh measure. Had he been in England, he would never have been locked up, or probably heard of again. I may note that, though evidently very tired, he was able to walk from one place to the other—altogether a considerable distance—and climb the steep Castlehill, as well as a flight of ninety-two steps to his cell in the Vestner Thurm.[1] Yet President von Feuerbach, in his *History of a Crime against a Human Soul*, the eloquent treatise that set all Germany ablaze with indignation, declares he was found in the street tottering and reeling like a drunken man, and scarcely able to stand upright.

By this time the lad was heartily frightened, and would hardly open his lips, though he wrote down his name when desired to do so. His pockets were searched, but they contained only a rosary, a worn-out key, a prayer-book, and some religious tracts and leaflets. He pretended not to understand the questions put to him, and appeared so impenetrably dense and stupid that Feuerbach described his condition as little different from that of an animal. But he kept his eyes and ears well open, and the warder in charge was not long in discovering that he was

[1] This account is derived from the official depositions taken by the police, which were suppressed by Feuerbach as wholly misleading. He more than once said to my father, "Any one who reads the Nuremberg archives would take Kaspar Hauser to be an impostor!" and once added emphatically, "They ought to be burnt." Strange to say, they actually *had* disappeared in 1883, nor was their disappearance ever accounted for. (See Appendix, p. 91.)

remarkably sharp-witted. Meanwhile his story spread like wildfire in the town, and, embellished with some additions and improvements, speedily developed into a popular romance.

A wild, or half-wild, man was said to be imprisoned in the Castle. People flocked to see him in his cell till, as one of the officers of the local gendarmerie, Major Hickel, writes on June 18, "it resembled a miracle-working shrine," and no place of pilgrimage was ever more zealously frequented. Not only the idle and curious, but men of science and men of letters, grave doctors and learned professors—not to speak of crowds of ladies bringing him toys—came, often from a great distance, to examine and talk him over. They discussed him in his presence with perfect unreserve, as he was not supposed to comprehend what passed; and he heard all kinds of fanciful surmises and theories as to his origin and past life. No doubt the strange story he told was in part suggested to him.

His first paroxysm of fear (when he came to the Castle he shrank back in terror even from the warder's little two-year-old boy) soon subsided, though he always remained excessively timid. By degrees his shyness wore off; he began to talk; to answer questions; and at last to unfold the marvellous tale that made so extraordinary a sensation.

All his life, he said, had been spent in a cell 6 or 7 feet long, 4 feet wide, and 5 feet high ; and always in a sitting posture : the only change in which was that when awake he sat upright, but leant back on a truss of straw when he slept. There were two small windows, but they were both boarded up ; and, as it was always twilight, he never knew the difference between day and night. Nor did he ever feel either hot or cold. He saw no one, and no sound of any kind ever reached his ear. Each morning, when he woke, he found a pitcher of water and a loaf of rye bread by his side. He was often thirsty, and when he had emptied his pitcher, used to watch to see whether the water would come again, as he had no idea how it was brought there. Sometimes it tasted strangely, and made him feel sleepy. He had toys to play with—two wooden horses and a wooden dog—and spent his time in rolling them about, and dressing them up with ribbons.

One day, a stool was placed across his knees, with a piece of paper upon it ; an arm was stretched out over his shoulder, a pencil put into his hand, and it was taken hold of, and guided over the paper. " I never looked round to see whom the arm belonged to. Why should I? I had no conception of any other creature beside myself." This was repeated seven or eight times; the arm was then withdrawn, but the stool, pencil, and paper left behind. He tried to copy the letters he had been made to trace, and, pleased with this new occupation, persevered till he had succeeded. Thus it was that he learned to write his name.

About three days afterwards (as far as he could judge) the man came again, and brought a little book—the same prayer-book that was found in his pocket. This was placed on his knees, and his hand laid upon it; then, pointing to one of the wooden horses, the man kept on repeating the word "Ross" (horse) till he had learned to say it after him. I should observe that, according to his own account, this was the first time in his life he had ever heard a sound of any kind, as the man came and went noiselessly. Then, in the same fashion, he was taught two sentences—

"In the big village, where my father is, I shall get a fine horse."

"I want to be a trooper, as my father was "— which he repeated by rote, of course without understanding them. When his lesson was learnt, the man went away, and he began

the same threat; and then the same rest on the ground, with "something soft" under his cheek. This pillow was evidently a comfort, as its mention is never omitted. By degrees he began to walk alone, supported by the man's arm, though at first only six steps at a time. The sunshine and fresh air together dazzled and bewildered him, and he scarcely took note where they went. They never travelled on a beaten track, but generally on soft sand; never went up or down hill, or crossed a stream. Sometimes he attempted to look about him; then the man instantly desired him to hold his head down. His clothes were once more changed; but the man, even while dressing him, stood behind him, so that he might not see his face. The two sentences he had learned were again and again impressed on his memory as he went along, the man always adding impressively, "Mind this well." He also said, "When you are a trooper, like your father, I will come and fetch you again." The journey cannot have been a long one, as he only took food once; he himself computed it had lasted a day and a night. Finally, the letter was put into his hands, with the words, "Go there—where the letter belongs"; and the man suddenly vanished from his side. He found himself alone in the street at Nuremberg—having never, till then, perceived that he had entered the town, or, in fact, seen it at all. He was quite dazed and helpless ; but some one kindly came and took charge of him and his letter.

This is, word for word, the narrative that was written down by Kaspar Hauser, and repeated by him before a specially appointed Commission of the magistrates of Nuremberg, in November 1828 ; though I must premise that he was never once examined on oath. It is, in every sense of the word, a marvellous story ; and yet, to my mind, the chief marvel of it is how any one should have been found able to believe it. That a lad who had spent his life sitting on the floor could have been able to stand on his feet at all, still less to have learned to walk within twenty-four hours, is not more impossible than that he could have been taught to write and speak, if only a few words, in two lessons. Even those who gave him full credit for honesty and integrity must have believed that his undeveloped mind had confused times and dates. Again, is it credible that no sound should ever have reached him in his cell, not even thunder? yet he expressed great terror at the first thunderstorm he witnessed in the Castle. Feuerbach attempted to explain this by sup-

posing him to be so taken up with his toys that
he could attend to nothing else. This was, as
my father said, comparing him to Archimedes,
absorbed in the solution of a problem. Kaspar
himself, when pressed, even by partial friends,
to explain any discrepancies or improbabilities
in his statements, used to declare such cross-
questioning made his head ache ; or else boldly
asserted, " I never said it."

One fact, however, remains undoubted—that
the story, such as it was, was very generally
accepted, and produced an almost unprecedented
impression. It appealed irresistibly to the imagination and the feelings of the hearers ; and,
spreading far and wide through the country,
aroused a perfect fever of sympathy and indignation. Many corroborative circumstances were
discovered and announced. Kaspar's eyes could
not bear the light ;[1] he had to be led up and
down stairs ; the soles of his feet were as soft
and tender as a child's palm (this the warder contradicted, declaring he suffered only from tight
boots) (see p. 101), etc. All adverse evidence

---

[1] This was certainly not the case on his first arrival ;
(see the evidence of Police-Corporal Wüst, p. 99) nor
does it agree with that of the warder, who states that, on
the second day of his imprisonment, he, in his childish
wonder and ignorance, thrust his finger into the flame of a
splinter of burning wood.

was discarded ; the men to whom Kaspar had
spoken at his first coming were bullied and disbelieved ; the guide who had led him to the
Neue Thor, he declined to recognise when
brought face to face with him.    Doctors were
sent to examine him, and pronounced him a
psychological curiosity—an " animal-man," who
had been evidently shut out from all communion
with his kind, whose faculties were dormant,
but whose senses were morbidly acute.    His
ears were so sensitive that every sound pained
them ;  though  fond  of  music,  he  suffered
greatly from pianoforte-playing ; and he could
not hear the regimental band without being
ill for two days afterwards.    A trumpet-call
threw him into a violent perspiration.    He
could see in the dark as well as by day, but
could not endure the light of the sun, and had
to wear a shade out of doors, and keep the
window-curtains always drawn in his room.
His sense of smell was extraordinary ; the scent
of the leaves of a walnut tree in a neighbouring
garden gave him the headache, and that of all
flowers, especially roses, was particularly dis-
agreeable to him.    Once, when approaching
the cemetery at Nuremberg, he perceived, even
at the distance of several hundred yards, a smell
so overpowering, that it almost threw him into

convulsions! Then there was a malconformation of the knees [1]—by no means peculiar to
himself—which was adduced as a proof that he
must always have sat with his legs stretched out
before him. Yet, on his arrival, he had coiled
himself up in the straw (see p. 3), and, according to the Castle warder, was in the habit not
only of sleeping with his feet drawn up, but
of tucking them under him, like a tailor, when
he sat (see p. 101). They found old scars
on his head and legs, proving that the poor boy
had, at some time or other, been cruelly mal-
treated; but these are not commented upon in
their report. One more recent hurt in the arm
had, Kaspar explained, been caused by "the
smart blow with the stick" he had received in
his cell. His body was well nourished, but it
is clear he had lived on bread and water; for
many weeks any other kind of food made him
sick, and it was not till the following October
that he was able to touch meat.[2] He never
learned to like either wine or beer.

[1] The patella, or knee-pan, which, in most cases, when
the leg is extended shows a slight projection, in his case lay
in a hollow; so that, when he sat on the ground with his leg
stretched out before him, the knee-joint rested on the floor.
Not even a card, it was said, could be inserted under it.

[2] According to Dr. Eckart, an army surgeon, this is a
not altogether uncommon experience with recruits from
the poorer districts of Bavaria.

All this time the police had been very busy searching and inquiring in every direction for any boy answering Kaspar's description that had been missing from his home. But they scoured the country in vain for any trace of one. No such boy was lost or known of. No one came forward to claim him; and in July 1828 he was formally adopted by the town of Nuremberg; an annual sum of 300 florins was voted for his maintenance and education, and he was placed under the charge of Professor Daumer.

His education had already been undertaken in the Castle, and he learned whatever he was taught well and quickly, though never afterwards with quite the same marvellous and rather suspicious facility he had shown in reading and writing. But Professor Daumer found that the constant influx of visitors seriously interfered with his lessons; and it was decreed that none should be admitted in future. He was, however, freely allowed to go out and see his friends; to drive with ladies on the summer afternoons, and attend assemblies in the evenings. He became the idol of Nuremberg society. Wherever he went, he was surrounded by a circle of admirers, while the genealogy of every reigning house in Germany was discussed and dissected in his presence, with the view of affiliating him to one of them. Nor were the great nobles of the land neglected. "Every door was knocked at" where it was hoped he might gain admittance. An accidental resemblance he bore to a daughter of the Grand Duchess Stéphanie of Baden led to the persistent belief that he was one of the two sons she had lost in their infancy, and, as it was now alleged, under suspicious circumstances. (See pp. 45, 71, etc.)

One cannot wonder that, flattered and caressed as he was, the boy's head should have been turned. He accepted the part assigned to him, and enacted the prince in disguise with success and complacency. He had the facile gift of readily adapting himself to his surroundings, knew how to conciliate and please them, and never seemed at a loss under any circumstances. His tutor, too, was delighted with him. The Professor was a zealous disciple of Hahnemann, and tried various homœopathic experiments on Kaspar, who proved an admirable subject. Some of the results he published are very amusing. The millionth part of the slightest infusion of medicine, dissolved in a glass of water, was plainly perceptible to Kaspar even at some distance, by its smell ; and not one smell only, but three "well-defined and

genuine" smells—the first sweet, the second
spirituous, the third "indescribable." The mere
touch of a closed medicine glass cured any
external hurt, and affected him for months
together; while he became intoxicated from
swallowing a single grape! Then he had
magnetic qualities. Iron attracted him; he
declared that in riding (among other accom-
plishments, he was being taught to ride), the
iron in the saddle kept him in his seat, while
his feet were held fast by the stirrups. But
when he wore spurs, his feet were distinctly
dragged in an opposite direction. Silver spurs
acted more powerfully than brass ones; and
the use of a silver spoon brought on such
violent tremblings that he was scarcely able to
raise it to his mouth, and Daumer compassionately bought him a wooden one. On one
occasion, when a man carrying a bag of money
came into the room in which he was, he had to
leave it in great perturbation, and wipe the
sweat off his brow in an adjoining one. Gold,
platina, diamonds, quicksilver, and magnets had
all a surprising effect upon him, creating a
variety of cold blasts. He discerned a pocket
mirror, of which the back was turned towards
him, at the distance of nine paces; *felt* the
sulphur on a match at the distance of two, and

distinguished metals hidden beneath a sheet of paper by merely holding his finger over them. A needle forgotten under the tablecover was brought to light by the sensation of chill it caused him. I may note that it was chiefly on Daumer's publication that President von Feuerbach relied in writing his book.

Notwithstanding these marvellous experiences, the interest felt in Kaspar Hauser began to flag in the course of the ensuing year. As time went on, the flood of popular enthusiasm visibly subsided; faults hitherto unsuspected began to be discerned in him; and it leaked out that he was cunning and untruthful. The sceptics, hitherto in a forlorn minority, and regarded rather in the light of black sheep, began to hold up their heads. Then suddenly, on October 17, the town was electrified by the news that Kaspar Hauser's life had been attempted, in broad daylight, and actually under his tutor's roof. At the usual dinner hour (12 o'clock) he had not made his appearance, and when searched for was found crouching in a corner of the cellar, bleeding from a cut across the forehead. Happily the wound proved very slight; but he was delirious for forty-eight hours, and had to be held down in his bed.

His evidence could consequently only be

taken on the 19th. He deposed that he had
been oppressed by forebodings for several pre-
vious days. On the morning of the 17th he
had gone first to the market with Fräulein
Kathi (Daumer) and then to Dr. Preu, who
gave him a walnut to eat; but, though he
scarcely took as much as a fourth part of it,
this made him so unwell (there spoke Daumer's
disciple) that he went home at once. It was
there, between 11 and 12 o'clock, that, while
in the closet, he was suddenly confronted by a
man with a black handkerchief drawn across his
face, who aimed a blow at him with a heavy
woodman's knife, crying, "After all, you will
have to die before you leave Nuremberg!"
The words gave him a shock which he felt in
all his limbs, for he recognised the voice of the
man who had brought him to the town. He
then lost consciousness. When he came to himself his first thought was to go to "Mother"
(as he used to call Frau Daumer), but in his
hurry and terror he mistook the way, turned
down instead of upstairs, and hid himself in the
cellar. He described the man accurately; his
height, his broad shoulders, his dark clothes, his
bran new shiny boots, and lemon-coloured kid
gloves.

How had this man made his way into the

house? There could be no question of the complicity of servants, for the Daumers kept none. The house door, generally fastened, might by chance have been left ajar. Kaspar (but no one else) heard the door-bell ring, very slightly, and called out to Kathi to go to the door.

Such an audacious attempt had never before been heard of, and the consternation was very great. Every imaginable effort was made to trace the murderer, but he had disappeared as if by magic. No such person had been seen either entering or leaving the town by the soldiers on duty at any of the gates, nor, though he must have passed through the streets at midday, had any one met him. One woman had seen a man leave the house at a quarter past eleven ; but this proved to be a beggar, to whom a charitable washerwoman had given a penny. Another saw a man washing his hands in a street trough hard by, but his appearance in no wise corresponded with that of the well-dressed individual in shiny black boots and lemon kid gloves.

The matter was vigorously taken up by the authorities, and nothing that it was possible to do was left undone, either in Nuremberg or in the neighbourhood. The town was subjected

to the most rigid scrutiny and vigilant supervision ; and Major Hickel tells us that within
a circuit of twenty-five miles round he caused
every inn, mill, outlying building, barn, stable,
or possible hiding - place to be searched, the
roads to be strictly patrolled, and notices to be
posted up at every police-station in the king-
dom. Yet nothing whatever was brought to
light.

When all his efforts proved fruitless, the
baffled Major began to ask himself whether such
a person as this invisible criminal really existed?
Was it likely that any man, not altogether out
of his senses, would choose such a time and place
for an assassination? would come into an in-
habited house, shortly before the dinner hour,
when all the inmates would assemble, and ring
at the door for admission? Was it possible
that, seen only for one brief and agonised
moment, his appearance could have been so
exactly noted, even to his shiny boots and lemon
kid gloves?[1] Would such a formidable weapon
as Kaspar described have inflicted only so insignificant a wound? and would the murderer, when he
saw his victim fall fainting at his feet, have for-

---

[1] Kaspar actually told my father that he had perceived
a ring on the man's hand, from the bulging of the fore-
finger of his glove !

borne to deal a second more decisive blow?
Might not Kaspar, bitterly feeling his position
as a dethroned hero, have sought to stimulate
the flagging interest of the public by a new and
romantic incident? This theory gained considerable credence in the town ; and when viewed
by the light of after events, must certainly be
accepted as the true one. The only difficulty
lies in believing that a timorous youth, who
"trembled like a leaf" on the slightest pro-
vocation, should have mustered courage to cut
himself with a knife. But he may not have
been as timid as he appeared. He certainly was
no coward on horseback.

From that time forward he was watched and
guarded by two police soldiers ; and till May
1831—a period of seventeen months—never
once left the house without their attendance.

Professor Daumer now asked to be relieved
of his charge. He had discovered that his pupil
was a confirmed liar ; or, as he himself expressed
it in a subsequent letter, "that Kaspar Hauser's
nature had lost much of its original purity, and
that a highly regrettable tendency to untruthfulness and dissimulation had manifested itself."
On the very morning of the day that Kaspar
received his wound, they had had a very bitter
quarrel. A friend had informed the Professor

that he had seen the lad gallivanting outside the
town, when he ought to have been busy with a
lesson he had been sent out to take. He was
taxed with this, and obstinately denied it, even
boldly declaring that the Professor might inquire
whether he did not speak the truth. The
Professor *did* inquire, and discovered that not
only on that day, but during the whole of the
week, Kaspar had absented himself from his
lesson. Daumer was excessively angry, for it
was by no means the first time he had found
himself deceived. He lectured his pupil most
severely, represented to him in the strongest
language all the evil consequences of deceit ;
then turned his back upon him, and sent him
word through Frau Daumer that a liar must be
treated with contempt and never noticed, and
that he himself should take measures to get rid
of him. Shortly after this he left the house, and
on his return found Kaspar wounded and
bleeding.

Freiherr von Tucher, who had always taken
a warm interest in the youth, was now appointed
his guardian, and he was placed in the house of
a Nuremberg trader named Biberbach, whose
sympathy took the practical form of receiving
him without payment. But here he only remained a few months. Biberbach and his wife

were soon disgusted with their charge. "How many bitter hours," writes Frau Biberbach, "what anguish and annoyance, Hauser caused us by his terrible untruthfulness, no official report has ever made known. After each painful scene of exposure, he used to promise amendment, and was always forgiven and taken back to our hearts as before : but the lying spirit could not be exorcised, and Hauser became more and more deceitful." Nor did he always profess penitence. Once, when taxed with "a cunningly contrived lie," he suddenly became violent, struck the table with his clenched fists, and passionately cried, "Then I would rather not live!" This time he had shirked his Latin lesson, and been overwhelmingly and completely convicted of falsehood. Herr Biberbach, for his part, was full of indignation. He told Kaspar, that after such misconduct he would not be allowed to go and dine at the Burgomaster's, as he generally did on that day every week, and that he was not to leave his room until further notice. But scarcely had Biberbach himself gone away, than the two police soldiers appointed to guard Kaspar heard a shot fired in his room, and, rushing in, found him lying on the floor senseless and bleeding, with the discharged pistol by his side. One of them hurried off to the police station, and

breathlessly announced that Kaspar had attempted to destroy himself.   Meanwhile, however, Kaspar had recovered his consciousness,
and explained that it was only an accident.
Some shelves had been fixed high up on the wall
of his room, and under them hung a brace of
pistols, kept loaded "for his better security."
On the topmost shelf were some books ; and
Kaspar had mounted a chair to reach down one
of them, when the chair suddenly slipped from
under him.   He stretched out his hands to save
himself, and inadvertently clutched hold of one
of the pistols, detached it from the wall, and
accidentally discharged it as he fell.   The bullet
had fortunately only grazed his temple.   He
had been practising at a mark with these pistols
during the autumn, but now begged they might
be taken away, and never brought back to his
room.

After this scene, it is not surprising to hear
that Herr Biberbach's "urgent private affairs
prevented him from retaining Kaspar Hauser
any longer under his roof."

Freiherr von Tucher now took him into his
own house, where he remained for eighteen
months.   His guardian's report is on the whole
a favourable, and, from the point of view taken,
a very sensible one.   He found Kaspar amiable,

tractable, anxious to learn, and extremely intelligent. He instances the power he had of
insinuating himself with those he wished to
please, and his "wonderful" skill and adroitness
in discerning and making use of their foibles.
He believed that the evil germ of a "most
regrettable moral corruption" had been implanted
by the foolish adulation and attention he had
received during the first few months, and that
his inordinate vanity, duplicity, and dissimulation were quite foreign to the simplicity of his
original character. He was firmly persuaded
that Kaspar had come to Nuremberg the "half-
animal" child of nature described, and conscientiously set to work to cure him of the faults
he had unhappily acquired.

It was at this time (in 1830) that the first
of the twenty-five pamphlets treating of the
"remarkable Nuremberg foundling" made its
appearance; and the rest followed in rapid
succession. One writer advocated a general
subscription on his behalf, and proposed to
appeal to every country in Europe. Another
(a Berlin police director) suggested that he
might be a truant school-boy, who had read
sensational stories, and run away from his friends
to become a cavalry soldier. This called forth
a host of controversial champions; but it was

not till 1832 that President von Feuerbach
published his *History of a Crime against a Human
Soul* that moved all hearts by its pathos and
eloquence.[1] To some of the later pamphlets I
shall have occasion presently to refer (see pp. 66–
87).

My father (Lord Stanhope) first made
Kaspar Hauser's acquaintance in the spring of
the preceding year. Shortly after the attempt
of October 17, 1829, he had been detained for
some days at Nuremberg, by an accident to his
carriage, and found every tongue busy with the
mysterious foundling who had so narrowly
escaped assassination. He heard the story with
the greatest interest, and expressed a wish to see
Kaspar : but at that time all visitors were rigidly
excluded. When, in May 1831, he was again
at Nuremberg, he renewed his request, met the
lad at the house of the Burgomaster, and was
singularly attracted by his manner and conversation. No one could be more winning than
Kaspar when he exerted himself to please ; and
he completely won my father's heart. He saw
him constantly ; used to take him out driving,

---

[1] Yet, even before his death in 1833, the author was
troubled with doubts as to Kaspar's credibility, and said to
a friend, "After all, who knows but Feuerbach may have
written a romance in his old age ?"

and became more and more interested in him. Here, again, Kaspar instinctively found and touched the right chord—my father's quickly aroused sympathy and tender compassion. His heart yearned towards any fellow-creature who had suffered either oppression or injustice ; and he fully believed that a great wrong had been done in this case. Of course he did not credit the story exactly as it had been told ; he himself pointed out some of its inconsistencies and improbabilities ; but he accepted the doctors' *dictum* that, the lad's faculties being dormant, his mind then resembled that of a very young child, who could scarcely be held accountable for an incoherent and incomplete narrative. Of the truth of its main facts, he was, however, entirely convinced. He believed that Kaspar had been kept for years in confinement, and grossly neglected and misused, and that this, most probably, had been the work of some one whose interest it was to get rid of him. In fact, he persuaded himself that Kaspar was a despoiled and defrauded heir. He was surprised that no reward had been offered to obtain information, and generously presented a sum of 500 florins for this purpose, characteristically requesting that his name might not appear. The magistrates who issued the proclamation worded it,

however, more in the form of a demand for the
denunciation of some unknown criminals than
an inquiry; and he always believed that this
caused people to hang back who might else have
given information.  They were naturally afraid
of appearing connected with a crime.  Otherwise, it would have been extraordinary that no
neighbour or school-fellow should ever have
come forward to claim this money, even though
he had lived, as my father conjectured, in some
secluded and out-of-the-way village beyond the
Austrian frontier.  At all events, it never was
claimed, and at the end of two years, according
to my father's directions, reverted to Kaspar
Hauser himself.

In addition to this gift, my father defrayed
the expenses of a journey to Hungary, which it
was thought desirable that Kaspar should undertake.  It seems that a statement made the year
before by a Roman Catholic priest[1] had led to

---

[1] In 1830, one Müller, who had been a Protestant
clergyman, and was then a Roman Catholic priest,
denounced a Protestant clergyman named Wirth, resident
in Upper Austria, and Anna Dalbonn, a governess resident
at Pressburg, as cognisant of the incarceration of Kaspar
Hauser.  He stated that four or five years before, when he
was tutor in the family of Countess Maytheny, at Pesth,
these two persons, having discovered that he knew their
secret, threatened him, and offered him money not to
divulge it ; but that he had declared, in the presence of the

the inference that he was a Hungarian, and he was accordingly tested with some Polish and Hungarian words, several of which he recognised. Some, he said, he had heard from his nurse ; others—these were generally oaths—from the man who had brought him to Nuremberg. Above all, the name Posonbya (Pressburg) threw him almost into convulsions ; he declared, with floods of tears, that he remembered it well, and even thought he had heard some one say that his father was at Posonbya. He earnestly implored to be allowed to go there ; and it was fondly hoped that his memory might reawaken among the scenes in which his childhood had been spent. He was accordingly conducted to

Countess, that he would have nothing to do with them. The Countess and the governess, summoned before a Hungarian tribunal, both indignantly denied this story, and declared they had never even heard the name of Wirth. It came out that Müller had sought to revenge himself on the governess, to whom he attributed his dismissal by the Countess, and bitterly hated his former clerical brother. But a calumny, once spread, dies very hard. Poor Anna Dalbonn had fallen under suspicion, and found her occupation gone. She petitioned the Emperor for an official recognition of her innocence, which she obtained, but, nevertheless, sank into such deep poverty that she was nearly crazed before her former employer, Countess Palffy, succeeded in finding her a home. Nor did the matter end there as regarded the Countess herself ; for in the following year Kaspar Hauser actually recognised her name as that of his long-lost mother ! (See p. 38.)

Pressburg by Von Tucher and Major Hickel;
but he recognised nothing and nobody, and
could not make out a single word of the
language. The sudden appearance of the cholera
cut short their stay. On his way back, he was
shown the Esterházy picture gallery at Vienna,
and announced he had seen the original of one
of the portraits. But, on referring to the
catalogue, it was found that the Esterházy in
question had died in 1646.

The Major relates one ridiculous incident of
this journey. Von Tucher had noted Kaspar's
singular habit of dropping off asleep quite
suddenly ; and his sleep, often accompanied by
painful distortions and grimaces, was so profound
as to resemble a trance, from which it was
impossible to rouse him. This would, it was
felt, be most inconvenient on a journey undertaken for purposes of observation, and his
thoughtful guardian provided a box filled with
coriander, fennel, and aniseed, that were to be
eaten as a preventative. But, even with this, it
was only by persistent tickling that his com-
panions managed to keep him awake. At last
Hickel had a brilliant idea. He and Von
Tucher agreed never to mention his name to
each other while he was asleep. After a time
the bad habit left him, and it was observed that

he never once dropped asleep during the journey home, though he was once detected listening at the door.

My father's great interest in Kaspar was—strange to say—nowise lessened by this inauspicious journey. He was again at Nuremberg in September, as full of sympathy and kindness as ever, and Kaspar, on his part, professed the most unbounded gratitude and devotion. Herr von Tucher complained—probably not without reason—that his pupil was being spoiled, and had become fractious, unsettled, and discontented. He wrote a very explicit letter to my father, telling him that his kindness had fostered Kaspar's extraordinary vanity and self-conceit, and done much harm, and that he had been highly injudicious in treating him as a grown-up person, whereas, though a man in years (Kaspar was twenty), he was a boy of ten or twelve in understanding. Further, that Kaspar deceived him, and had been twice kicked out of respectable houses (Daumer's and Biberbach's), on account of his lies. He ended by declaring that my father must either take charge of Kaspar altogether, or else cease to see him ; in which latter case only would he consent to remain his guardian. This letter, though full of praises of his " rare goodness of heart," " wonder-

D

ful kindness " and " noble liberality," annoyed my father very much. Kaspar, too, complained bitterly of his guardian, who " wanted to make a bookbinder of him against his will." Finally, the Nuremberg authorities, taking up the cue, announced that they would no longer pay the 300 florins they had allowed him.[1]

I think that all, by general consent, now looked forward with hope to seeing their unwelcome charge taken off their hands. Had not an English noble—a rich English noble—taken a fancy to him? They had, it appears, an exalted idea of the wealth of our aristocracy. " This Earl," writes Von Tucher, " is reported to possess an income of £20,000 a year, but that is by no means a large fortune for a peer of Great Britain."

My father was made to feel himself the best, if not the last friend left to Kaspar in his pressing need ; most certainly the only friend able and willing to take charge of him ; and,

---

[1] They had already made an attempt to rid themselves of this obligation. In January 1830, when Von Tucher was appointed guardian, they requested him to appeal to the generosity of the king on their behalf, and have the payment transferred to the State. The Government refused, and expressed surprise at this petition, as the municipality had, in July 1828, voluntarily undertaken to provide for the education and maintenance of Kaspar Hauser.

moved to compassion by his forlorn condition, he in an evil hour consented. He did not, as has been sometimes averred, formally adopt Kaspar Hauser, but he made himself answerable for his personal safety, education, and maintenance as long as he himself lived, and engaged to furnish him with the means of subsistence by his will. He was to appoint any guardian or tutor he might select, and report, at least once a year, upon Kaspar's education to the appointed authorities. It was understood that the latter was to follow some profession, hereafter to be determined. In one of his subsequent letters to Dr. Meyer, my father says, "You well know that I did not wish to have Kaspar Hauser made over to me as a 'curiosity,' but I found his guardian unwilling to keep him, the town of Nuremberg disinclined to continue his allowance, and heard he was to be apprenticed to an artisan in the spring. I therefore took him under my protection, as a young man needing help, for whom I had a sincere liking, and who had always shown himself affectionate, teachable, and grateful to me. I did not then believe him to be as untrustworthy as various circumstances have since convinced me that he was; nor had he, up to that time, ever shown himself in an unfavourable light." Un-

fortunately, believing him to be strongly prejudiced, my father had never taken Von
Tucher's report into account. It must be
admitted that he made a great mistake, and that
it was heavily visited upon him ; for never,
surely, did an act of disinterested kindness bear
more bitter fruit.

Kaspar Hauser was formally handed over to
his new protector on November 26, 1831. All
was now jubilation and congratulation. The
King of Bavaria in person wrote to thank my
father for his "noble action." Troubles and
worries were set at rest, and every one was
pleased, for every one's object had been gained.
The one exception to the general satisfaction
was Freiherr von Tucher. He had rigidly and
conscientiously endeavoured to do his duty, and
was naturally aggrieved by the angry complaints
of his pupil, and the opinion expressed both by
my father and Von Feuerbach, that he had
misunderstood and mismanaged him. He had
previously thrown up his guardianship, and in
the following month Kaspar was placed under
the care of Dr. Meyer, a school-teacher at Ansbach, where my father left him when he returned
to England in January 1832. Major, now
Lieutenant-Colonel Hickel, was appointed
curator, and the Burgomaster of Nuremberg

guardian, but the latter was replaced for the time by President von Feuerbach.

Kaspar, emancipated from Von Tucher and the Latin grammar, thoroughly enjoyed his new position. He half fancied himself an English nobleman by adoption, and in fact was called "My Lord" by some of his friends. He anxiously looked forward to joining the family circle in England, anticipated the brilliant position he would occupy in London society, and even took an intelligent interest in English politics. Nevertheless, he had not discarded his favourite *rôle* of a Hungarian magnate.

I should have mentioned that among the tests applied to him in 1830 was a catalogue of Hungarian Christian names, and he had at once picked out Istan (Stephen) as his own. He frequently told my father that he remembered being called Istan when he was a child. "Another name," he added, "ought to follow, but, try as I will, for the life of me I cannot recall it!" He had likewise some recollection of his father's castle. Once, indeed, he saw it in a dream, and was able to describe it minutely, even to the furniture of the rooms.

During the preceding month of October, Ladislaus von Merey, a Hungarian noble, passing through Nuremberg with his son and his

son's tutor, asked to speak to Kaspar alone.
He wanted to find out whether he understood
Slavonic, a language spoken in a part of the
country with which he himself was well acquainted, and where the governess Dalbonn had
at one time lived.  Kaspar was taken to see
him, and knew no Slavonic.  But when he said
in Hungarian, " Istan goes to Szalakusz " (the
castle of Countess Maytheny), Kaspar appeared
to receive an electric shock ; he became fright-
fully agitated, and, gesticulating more wildly
than he had ever done before, cried, " Yes !
yes ! that's it !  That's what I have been searching for so long !"  The name of Bartakowich
(Countess Maytheny's maiden name) was then
mentioned, and he screamed aloud, as if panic-
struck, " That is my mother !"  His excite-
ment and agitation almost amounted to frenzy,
and became so uncontrollable that the Hungarian, alarmed for the consequences, hurriedly
sent him home.  Yet when my father, shortly
afterwards, questioned him as to the name
that had caused such violent emotion, he had
already forgotten it ; and this strange lapse of
memory was set down to the fearful shock his
system had undergone ! [1]

[1] My father confessed to having been surprised, and also
to having wondered that a very young child, such as

The two names had, however, been carefully noted, and it was thought that the key to the enigma had at last been found. My father decided that an investigation should be carried on in the district indicated ; and he asked Colonel Hickel to accept this delicate mission. He was to inquire into Müller's allegations on the spot, and, if possible, see both him and Dalbonn. Accordingly, in February 1832, he obtained a three months' leave of absence, "in order to travel, at Earl Stanhope's expense, in Hungary." He traced Müller with great difficulty, and heard a bad account of him. Madame Dalbonn he met at the house of the Countess P——— (evidently Palffy). The castle of Szalakusz and the Countess Maytheny were easily found, but after the most searching inquiries and a careful investigation of the family history in all its circumstances, he came to the conclusion that nothing whatever was to be done for Kaspar in Hungary. For one thing, there was no inheritance to dispute. The report which he forwarded to my father in May definitively closed all prospects in that quarter.

My father was not only disappointed, but dismayed. If the whole story was false, how was

Kaspar must then have been, should have known its mother only by her maiden name.

he to account for the thrilling and dramatic scene with the Hungarian gentleman[1] at Nuremberg? What could it be but a consummate piece of acting on Kaspar's part? For the first time, as he tells us, the question crossed his mind—Was this plausible, docile, affectionate young man to be depended upon? The doubt, once entertained, developed with alarming rapidity as various trifling and hitherto unheeded incidents and little fibs recurred to his memory. He was, besides, greatly distressed on hearing, soon after, that Hickel's mission and its object had become known in the locality, and that the family in question were justly offended at the imputations on their character these inquiries had implied.

Nor were Meyer's reports eminently satisfactory. He found Kaspar more backward than he had expected, and certainly not so willing to learn. His application was only by fits and starts, never continuous; and he was too fond of asking, "What good is this to do me?" He showed no aptitude for any profession, and trade was not to be thought of now

---

[1] He was afterwards told that this Hungarian noble and his son had since often laughed together over the "startling dramatic entertainment" got up for their benefit by Hauser.

that he had been introduced into a different
sphere. Perhaps he might do best as a clerk.
His inordinate vanity and self-conceit were not
surprising, in consideration of the flattering
attentions he had been in the habit of receiving,
and now received more than ever. His tendency was to be shifty and untruthful.

In a report furnished to the police authorities
in 1834, Meyer gives a curious picture of Kaspar's
powers of dissimulation. He was so different at
different times that no one could have believed
him to be the same person ; and Feuerbach well
described his nature as " chameleon like." The
every-day face, which he wore to those im-
mediately about him, was neutral and commonplace enough, but instantly vanished if he was
in company. Sometimes, when surprised sitting
alone in his own room, it was gloomy and morose,
and looked years older : then changed as if by
magic when he saw himself observed. It could
wear whatever expression seemed appropriate to
the occasion : sometimes the candid simplicity
and ignorance of a little child ; sometimes the
bright intelligence of an appreciative listener ;
now it beamed with affection and sympathy, and
then again, when he was reproved or angered,
bore the unmistakable stamp of an evil and vin-
dictive temper. To those he was anxious to

please he was perfectly charming : no manner
could be more insinuating, coaxing, and caressing,
no words more winning and sympathetic. He
had a singular power of assimilating himself to
his surroundings, and of knowing and doing
exactly what they expected of him. He was
very soft-hearted ; his tears were ever ready to
flow ; but Meyer disliked these lachrymose
exhibitions, and once, when he began weeping
bitterly at an account of the Deluge, severely
said, " This must not happen again." Nor did
it, though, as Meyer rather plaintively adds :
" I read many other more moving passages with
much pathos." He would never tell the truth.
" To lie had become so completely a second
nature with him, that it was exacting an actual
impossibility to require him to give it up." Yet
he was extremely touchy whenever his veracity
was in question. Though he constantly made
statements and framed excuses that could easily
and demonstrably be proved false, he was in-
variably most indignant when found out, and
insisted on his word being taken in the teeth of
all adverse evidence. As these continual wrangles
could do no possible good, Meyer came to the
wise conclusion that it was useless to persist in
taxing him with every petty falsehood that passed
his lips, and ignored all lies, except in case of

actual necessity. After this their relations became far more comfortable, and Kaspar was always (with the exception of an occasional fit of sullenness) friendly and civil to his tutor. But he took a violent dislike to Colonel Hickel. Once they had a regular passage-at-arms together, during which the Colonel, whose temper appears to have been short, became so exasperated by his prevarications that he with difficulty refrained from boxing his ears. Kaspar, equally excited, twice repeated, " Then I would rather die ! " his favourite asseveration whenever he found himself disbelieved. " By all means ! " retorted the angry Colonel ; " die, then, and we will inscribe on your tombstone, ' Here lies the deceiver Kaspar Hauser.' " When, soon after, he was away for a few days, the young man sought to revenge himself by making mischief between him and the President. On his return home, Feuerbach told him of this, adding, " That lad frightens me ! Why, he is a regular intriguer and backbiter ! Can this be our Kaspar Hauser ? "

But when his own personality was not in question, he was neither unfair nor unkind. He was very popular in society, making many friends, and the advice he gave them was always sound, sensible, and well meant. He had a wonderful

insight into character, and read men's minds as
he would an open book ; always judged correctly,
and divined motives and foresaw actions with an
accuracy that amazed and alarmed Meyer. He
was a shrewd and intensely suspicious observer,
and had an inconvenient knack of finding out
everything that it was wished to keep secret from
him. Any plan or arrangement regarding himself he knew, in spite of all precautions, as soon
as it was made. He received his numerous
visitors with tact and discrimination, always
making a favourable impression, and yet manag-
ing to cut short any uninteresting or unimportant
call. In September 1833, when passing through
Nuremberg on his return from a tour in Saxon
Switzerland, he was, at her own request, presented
to the Queen of Bavaria, and showed neither
awkwardness nor embarrassment. He presented
one of his paintings, and begged Her Majesty
to proclaim an amnesty for the man that had
kept him prisoner, as the only chance of protect-
ing him from the assaults of murderers.

He had apparently not adopted a strange
theory, propounded by Feuerbach in a pamphlet
published nine months before, that this gaoler
had in reality been his benefactor. According
to Feuerbach's conjecture, Kaspar was the legiti-
mate son of a sovereign House, who stood in the

way of the next in succession, and would have
been long since in his grave, had he not been
rescued by a faithful retainer, who kept him in
close confinement to conceal him from his pur-
suers. The House designated was the reigning
House of Baden,[1] and the " Memoir " was dedi-

[1] The myth of a suppressed Prince of Baden had already
been ventilated in the daily papers. Kaspar was reported
to be the son and heir of the Grand-Duke Charles Louis
Frederick and his French wife Stéphanie de la Pagerie,
the adopted daughter of Napoleon : a little prince, born in
1812, who only lived a fortnight. He did not, it was
alleged, really die, but was secretly carried off, and a dying
baby left in his place, to make room for the succession of a
wicked uncle, the next Grand-Duke. A certain Countess
Hochberg was accused of having accomplished this substitution in the disguise of the White Lady of Baden ; and
Major Hennenhofer was named as her accomplice. It is,
I believe, quite true that the Grand-Duchess, who was very
ill at the time, never saw her dead child ; but it is hard to
conceive that its father, and its grandmother the Margravine,
who, with her daughter Amelia, was in close attendance,
together with the ten Court physicians assembled for the
*post-mortem* examination—of whom two had been present
at its birth—could have been deceived as to its identity.
Feuerbach had not ventured to publish any names, and
the whole story was first openly promulgated in a pamphlet
published at Stuttgart the year after Kaspar's death. It was
revived again and again, and was said to be credited by the
Grand-Duchess herself. She had read and admired Feuerbach's *Crime against a Human Soul;* she told my father
she would have liked to translate it into French ; and she
often questioned him about Kaspar Hauser. But if the
idea that this phenomenal being might be her own child
ever crossed her mind, it was promptly discarded as an
" impossibility." The Duchess of Hamilton (Princess Marie

cated to a Princess of Baden : Caroline, Queen
Dowager of Bavaria. Of course he could
produce no evidence in support of this romantic
tale ; it rested only on " coincidence of circumstances," " strong presumptions," and Kaspar's
own "remarkable dreams " (!), which together
constituted what he is pleased to call a "moral
certainty."

President von Feuerbach died of a paralytic
stroke on May 28 of the same year (1833) ;
and my father appointed Herr Hofrath (Court
Councillor) von Klüber guardian in his stead.
Like his predecessor, Von Klüber was a well-
known and highly distinguished man, but not,
like him, a resident at Ansbach ; and he selected
his friend, Herr Hofrath (Court Councillor)
Hofmann as his representative.   This gentleman
had always taken the liveliest interest in Kaspar's
story ; but on a nearer acquaintance did not
approve of him at all.   After giving him daily
instruction for six months, he said to Dr.
Meyer, " I can't get on with that young man.
I have no opinion of him ; I have found him
both a flatterer and a dissembler."

of Baden) wrote in 1872 that her mother had never believed
the story ; and Napoleon III. told King Louis of Bavaria,
who questioned him on the subject during his visit to
Paris in 1867, that Stéphanie had described it to him as a
" senseless myth."

On the occasion of Hofrath Hofmann's appointment, my father wrote to announce that, though doubts had latterly arisen in his mind as to Hauser's former unhappy position, they would in no wise affect his conduct. As before, he would provide what was needful for his maintenance and improvement, and had already, in case of his own death, secured him an annuity by a codicil to his will. Even without this, his heirs would have felt bound by the engagement he had entered into. He added that the best kindness to the young man would be the choice of some suitable profession for him.

This announcement was a great relief to all concerned. My father's letters had been full of doubts and questionings; and in the preceding autumn he had sent the President a list of thirty points that required elucidation in Kaspar's story. Meyer had become so anxious about his pupil's prospects, that he omitted, as far as possible, in his reports any mention of his deceitfulness, lest my father should be still further prejudiced against him. What would become of him if his kind and liberal patron were to give him up?

My father, as we have seen, had no such ungenerous intention. For a year past he had been revolving in his mind a most painful

problem—the question how far he had been
duped and deceived. The more he pondered
over Kaspar's story, the more he felt it to be
impossible and incredible, but he still believed
that he had been very badly treated, and was
willing to hope that his habits of duplicity and
dissimulation were contracted through fear of ill
usage. He even thought it possible that his life
had been threatened if he ventured to reveal
where he had been. He was ingenious in
finding excuses for the friendless lad towards
whom his heart had warmed, whom he had
taken under his wing, and found affectionate and
grateful. Never for one moment had he thought
of casting him adrift.

Kaspar's profession was now decided on ; he
was to be a clerk ; and in July he entered the
Ansbach Chancellerie as a paid writer. There
could be no further uneasiness as to his future,
which was securely provided for ; yet he was
profoundly dissatisfied. He was heartily weary
of his lessons, and gave less and less attention to
them : nor did he appreciate his position as a
clerk. He had hoped for something very
different, and bitterly and repeatedly complained
that he had not been taken to England. He
hated Hickel, and was sorely chafed by his
dependence upon him. " I can't stand the

Colonel any longer," he said, " I can't bear being
for ever told—' When the Earl comes, what will
he say?'" My father was again travelling in
Germany, and was expected at Ansbach for
Christmas. On December 9 (subsequent events
fixed the date indelibly on his memory), Meyer
had occasion to find great fault with his pupil,
and rated him severely. Kaspar was, as usual,
blameless, and fenced with his adversary till,
fairly driven into a corner, he began to cry and
promise to lie no more. Meyer was very angry
and spoke very strongly. " I wish," he cried,
" I had never set eyes on you! Through you I
have perhaps forfeited my character as an honest
man! Have I not, from an exaggerated regard
for your welfare, given a better report of you
than I ought to have done? and when the Earl
comes, how can I find it in my conscience not
to tell him the truth? What will happen then?
He already, as you well know, mistrusts you.
Consider the predicament you place me in!
Even here in the town you are discredited.
People have found you out, and there are few
indeed that still see in you the former upright,
amiable, good-natured Kaspar Hauser. How
must it all end if you go on like this?" Then
—for the hundredth time — he preached re-
pentance and amendment. Kaspar listened and

E

said nothing, but he was deeply incensed, and never after that would take Dr. Meyer's hand.

Then followed the catastrophe. On Saturday, December 14, as Meyer and his wife were sitting together in the short winter's afternoon, Kaspar rushed into the room, panting, speechless, and half frenzied, pointed with theatrical gestures to a wound in his breast, and, seizing Meyer's arm, dragged him out of the house. They hurried along in the direction of the Hofgarten (public gardens), and Meyer asked, "Was it there?" Kaspar nodded assent, and gasped out —"Went—Hofgarten—man—had knife—gave bag—stabbed—ran as hard as could—bag still lying there." Meyer, perceiving that his strength was fast failing, then induced him to turn back, and got him safely home, though he sank down once on the way. He was put to bed : two doctors were summoned, and Meyer rushed off to the police-bureau. A gendarme was instantly despatched to search the Hofgarten, and there picked up a silk bag, which contained the following note, written in pencil, and legible only in a mirror, as the handwriting was reversed :

" To be delivered.

" Hauser will be able to tell you exactly how I look, and whence I come.  To save Hauser the trouble I will myself tell you where I come from.

"I come from from . . .
" The Bavarian frontier . . .
" On the river . . .
" I will even give my name as well.

"M. L. OE."

There was no address.

The doctors meanwhile had examined Kaspar, and found a small cut on the left side of his breast, which, from its slanting direction, they were unable thoroughly to probe ; but it bled very slightly, and he was pronounced to be in no danger.  The Commissioners of Police even commenced taking his evidence, but were not allowed to proceed far.  The next day, as there was some fear of inflammation, they were not admitted at all; and it was only on the mornings of the 16th and 17th that his deposition could be taken.  He made it calmly and collectedly, but the doctors would not allow him to be sworn.

That Saturday morning, as he was entering his office about nine o'clock, he found a stranger in the blouse of a workman waiting for him, who brought a message from the Hofgärtner (head gardener), asking him to come to the

garden that afternoon at half-past three, and
see some specimens of clays from the borings of
the new artesian well. The same man had come
three days before with a similar request, to
which he had not then attended. This time he
answered, "I will come," and went. There
was no one at the artesian well, and he went a
little further on to the Uz monument (the
memorial of the poet Uz). There another taller
man started forward, put a bag into his hand,
saying, "I give you this," and, as he took it,
stabbed him in the breast. Kaspar dropped the
bag, and ran home as fast as his legs would
carry him,[1] without ever looking back or
noticing whom he met. The man was fifty or
thereabouts, tall, with a red face, and black
whiskers and moustache ; he wore a cloak and
a black hat. No one else was in the garden,
for it was a wild blustering afternoon, with
showers of snow and sleet. "Why," he was
asked, "when you found no one at the appointed
place, did you go on to the Uz monument?"
"Because it is my usual walk. I often walk
there." "After what happened at Nuremberg
were you not afraid?" "Now that I have a

---

[1] Kaspar had told Dr. Horlacher that he had swooned on
receiving the blow, and did not know how long he had lain
on the ground unconscious.

foster-father, I have no fear." It was pointed out to him that he had first said the messenger sent to him was fair, and then that he was dark. This, he insisted, could only be the mistake of the shorthand writer.

That same evening, at eight o'clock, the Commissioners were hurriedly sent for again, as his condition had suddenly changed for the worse, and he was not expected to survive the night. In fact, he died as the clock was striking ten, just seventy-eight hours after he had received his wound. About a dozen people, including the officials and three doctors—a fourth had previously left—were present in the room.

All his utterances during this last day were carefully noted down. His nurse deposed that he kept moving his hands over his bedclothes as if writing, muttering to himself, "I must write—I have much to write to-day—all in pencil." As another witness was putting his bed to rights, he suddenly flung out his arms, and with wide-open staring eyes cried, "My God! My God! To have to shuffle off like this, in shame and disgrace!" Once again he repeated these words in his nurse's hearing, and said, "What is written with lead, no one can read."

This was before the arrival of the Commissioners, who found him in a deep swoon.
When he came to himself, Meyer bade him put
his trust in God, and asked if he had any-
thing more to say. "I would—gladly forgive,"
he replied, "if I knew who—had done—this
—to me." Meyer resumed, "Dear Kaspar,
have you nothing to say to me? Look me full
in the face. You know that I have always
meant well by you." "Oh, much—very much
—I might have to say—but cannot"; then
taking Meyer's hand, he added, "Many—many
thanks—for all—you have done—I owe you
—more—than I can tell." Then he murmured
something about men being more easily led
away by evil than by good. "I—too—been
led away — but — found — the right road."
Colonel Hickel now came forward and asked,
"Have you no word for the Earl?"—"For
the Earl—yes—my thanks, too—many thanks.
He, too—must—keep on—the right road—
that the faults—from which—he—too, is not—
quite free—do not overcome—him. He has—
done good to—many—done—good to me, too
—in—the next world—will be—reckoned—or
it might—go ill, too——" His gasping utterances here ceased to be intelligible. A pause
followed. Then he muttered to himself, "Sin

—destruction—cannot get free—the monster—
stronger—than I"; and again became inaudible,
till, as if appealing to those around, he raised
his voice to say, "If you see—a man—leaving
—the right road—drag him back—at once—by
the hair of his head." Another pause, then
again, "Hard struggle—not every man—can—
endure it."

Pastor Fuhrmann, who had prepared him
for confirmation, and was praying by his bed-
side, asked him if his mind was at rest.

"Have I not," he answered, "begged pardon
—of every one—I know—why should I—not
be—at rest—the good God—surely—will not
forsake me."

"It is not enough," said the Pastor, "to ask
forgiveness. Our Lord has told us to forgive,
as we hope to be forgiven. There should be no
anger or rancour in your heart."

"Why should I—feel anger—or rancour—
no one—ever—did me wrong."

He was growing more and more feeble every
moment, and repeated several times, "Tired
—very tired—all my limbs—too heavy—for
me."

The good Pastor comforted and encouraged
him with the words of Scripture, ending with,
"Father, not my will," and Kaspar responded,

"but Thine be done." To test his consciousness, the Pastor asked, "Who prayed thus?" and again he was ready with his answer, "Our Saviour."—"And when?"—"Before He died." A few minutes after this followed his last words, "Tired—very tired—a long journey—to take," and, turning his face to the wall, he passed peacefully away.

The post-mortem examination[1] showed how far the doctors had at first been from estimating the extent of the injury. Not only had the knife passed through the lung, but its point had actually punctured the heart. They were at a loss to understand how Kaspar, after receiving such a wound, should have been able to go so long a distance : first to hurry home from the Hofgarten, then go nearly all the way back again, and lastly return home a second time. So far they were agreed ; but as to how this wound was inflicted, they held diametrically opposite opinions. Dr. Horlacher, who claimed a professional experience of forty-one years, believed that it had been dealt by Kaspar himself with his left hand (he was left-handed, and even played bowls with the left hand) ; while

[1] It is remarkable that, though the poor corpse was examined and described with almost painful minuteness, no mention was made of the malconformation of the knees (see p. 15).

Dr. Albert was convinced that he had been murdered. But where was the murderer?

The police-soldier sent to search the Hofgarten could only trace the footsteps of one man in the snow, who seemed to have been walking up and down ; there were none near the artesian well, nor in the direction of the gate leading into the country. What tracks there were were quickly obliterated by the people crowding to visit the spot, and by the snow which continued to fall all night. The knife was nowhere to be found, but might have been thrown into a little brook hard by. [1] Colonel Hickel, as he had done at Nuremberg, sent out notices to rouse the country, and made strict inquisition in the town ; for, as Kaspar had been invited to the Hofgarten three days before he went, it was concluded the murderer must then have been on the spot. Now, Ansbach is an insignificant provincial town, little visited by strangers, and least of all in the depth of winter ; the kind of place where a new face is in itself an event, and every newcomer is eagerly discussed ; yet no trace of any stranger was discoverable. Nor

---

[1] Several years afterwards a dagger or stiletto, such as might have caused the fatal wound, was dug up in the Hofgarten.

were the researches in the neighbourhood more
successful.

My father, who was then travelling, received
the news on Christmas Eve, at a post-station on
the road between Vienna and Munich. He
was greatly shocked, and no less surprised; for
having, as we have seen, made himself person-
ally responsible for Kaspar's safety, he had
taken every imaginable precaution to secure it.
"Had he been a State prisoner committed to
my charge," he writes to Dr. Meyer, "I could
not have guarded him with greater care and
anxiety. Feuerbach once said to me, 'You
cannot do more, short of locking him up.'"
No strangers were admitted to see him unless
they could produce a satisfactory guarantee of
their respectability. Kaspar was strictly forbidden to go out, even into the streets, by
himself; whenever he left the house he was to
be accompanied by an old soldier, who was a
servant of Colonel Hickel's; but this restriction
became excessively irksome to him, and he persuaded the President to relax it. He was then
allowed to go about alone in the streets, but
never outside the town, and the Hofgarten was
consequently forbidden ground.[1] "When once

[1] Before going to the Hofgarten on that fatal Saturday
afternoon, Kaspar visited Pastor Fuhrmann, and told him,

he was relieved of supervision in the streets, it was impossible to prevent his going elsewhere. This was done without my knowledge or consent, and I was only informed of it after Kaspar's death. On this occasion, as on many others, President von Feuerbach assumed a right to which he had no claim ; for all authority, and with it all responsibility, belonged to me alone."

On arriving at Munich, my father hastened to seek an audience of the King, as well as of the Minister of the Interior, and obtained the appointment of a Commission of Inquiry, and the proclamation of a reward of 10,000 florins for the apprehension of the murderer. The whole district, for many miles round, was again patrolled, the strangers' books at the inns, in which all wayfarers had to enter their names, carefully searched, and every carriage and cart that had been in use noted ; for those were not the days of railroads, and there was comparatively little travelling. Ansbach had no regular communication with the outer world except the Eilwagen (mail cart) that brought the daily post. But all this trouble was taken in vain.

as he left, that he was going on to Fräulein Lilla von Stichauer, who had asked him to come and help her to paste a cardboard screen that she was making. This was untrue : she had made no such appointment.

Moreover, many suspicious circumstances tended to confirm Colonel Hickel's firmly-rooted belief that the man in the cloak was a myth.

It was not likely that Kaspar would go out in very inclement weather merely to inspect specimens of clays ; for he had never shown the slightest interest in them, and they could not be novelties, as no work had been done at the artesian well since the preceding month of August.

He expressed the greatest eagerness to recover the bag dropped in the Hofgarten, yet never once inquired what it had been found to contain.

Dr. Meyer remembered to have seen a similar bag in his possession since his last visit to Munich, but none such was found among his effects.

The note was folded exactly in the way that Kaspar was accustomed to fold his notes.

It contained a fault in grammar he often made in his writings, the substitution of " den " for " dem."

The paper (of which the water-mark was cut off) corresponded with some found in his waste-paper basket.

For about three weeks before December 16, he had been in the habit of leaving the Chancellerie, on some pretext or other, before the right

time, and had always shut himself up in his
own room for an hour or more every day, locking the door, and pulling down the window-
blind, though it was dark winter weather.

Some letters and papers, known to have been
in his possession a short time before, were not
found after his death. Nor was a diary, that he
professed to have kept from the time he had
lived with Professor Daumer, forthcoming. He
had been very mysterious about this journal,
and never allowed any one to see it, but once
showed my father a blue paper cover, lying
in a drawer, which he said contained it.
There had been, at different times, great pressure brought upon him to produce it, but he
never would; and at last declared that he had
burnt it.

It was never supposed that Kaspar had
deliberately intended to commit suicide; but
that the pressure required to pierce his thick
winter clothing and wadded coat drove the knife
further home than he expected, and inflicted a
deadly, instead of a slight wound. The blow,
too, was dealt in a dangerous place; had it been
struck only a little lower down—under the next
rib—it would have done comparatively little
harm. It should be borne in mind that the
former attempt at Nuremberg had been a great

success. Why should it not be repeated? It
had reawakened the waning interest in his story,
replaced him on his pedestal as the hero of the
hour, removed him from a very distasteful
position, and confirmed the existence of a mysterious persecutor—the criminal "against a
Human Soul," which some had begun to doubt.
Who else could have any conceivable object
in seeking to take Kaspar's life? The story
and the murderer could not be dissociated;
they must either be accepted or rejected together.

The judicial investigation dragged on for
nine months. Not till September 1834 did
the Ansbach Commissioners announce that the
materials at hand for their inquiry were ex-
hausted, and proceed to make their fifth and final
report to the Minister of Justice at Munich.
At the end of February my father had gone to
Nuremberg to examine the witnesses who had
first seen Kaspar on his arrival—that is, the
two men whom he addressed in the street, the
Captain's groom, and the Captain himself; and
he also obtained the evidence of two police-
soldiers who were on guard at the police-station
when he was brought there. During the three
hours that he was detained, he never once
attempted to sit down, but either stood or

walked about (see p. 100); and one of these
men was positive that when asked where he
came from, he answered, "I must not tell."—
"Why not?"—"Because I don't know."

The communication addressed by my father
to Colonel Hickel on the subject induced the
Commissioners to order a formal and minute
re-examination of those witnesses whose evidence, as disproving Kaspar's story, is the first
point touched upon in their report. The
second is Dr. Meyer's long and detailed account
of his two years' experience of his pupil, and
the estimate he formed of his character, "cor-
roborated on many important points by the
testimony of Herr Biberbach, Professor Daumer,
and Freiherr von Tucher, even though they
differ in opinion as to whether Hauser inflicted
the wound himself."

The result of the inquiry was "the conviction irresistibly forced upon their minds," that
no murder had been committed. From first to
last, "no single ground of suspicion had arisen
against any individual that was not completely
set at rest by subsequent investigation; and,
after taking into account all the circumstances,
and more particularly the attempted murder at
Nuremberg," they had come to the above conclusion.

They had, "even in their first report, endeavoured to explain the reasons that had led
them to doubt the truth of Kaspar's account of
the pretended outrage, and given rise to the conjecture that he had dealt the blow himself."

Here follows a discussion of his character
and probable motives.

"From this point of view, three facts deserve more especial notice and consideration.

"When Kaspar no longer liked staying with
Daumer, because the latter had seen through
him, because his untruthfulness had been discovered and severely censured, when tutor and
pupil alike wished to part, there occurred the
first so-called attempt to murder, in broad
daylight, and in a frequented street, and the
murderer unaccountably disappears, leaving no
trace.

"After this attempt Kaspar was transferred
to the house of Herr Biberbach ; but here again
a similar motive led to similar results. Hauser
did not like this family. And—again at the
very nick of time—the accidental discharge of a
pistol in his own room, occasioning a slight
hurt, furthered his wish to leave the house.

"Then he came to Ansbach. Here, again, his
tutor found him out. He heard of the doubts
cast upon his story, and shared by Lord Stan-

hope. Fearing these doubts might lead to fresh researches, and perhaps unwelcome discoveries, discontented with his position and the occupation assigned to him, disliking work, severely taken to task for lies on December 9 —four days before the wound : his endeavour would be to put an end to this state of things at any price; and the supposed murder then occurs, in as marvellous a way as at Nuremberg, by daylight and in a public garden, and again the murderer vanishes, leaving a note and a bag, as if to scoff at the researches of the police.

"This note, in particular, should receive the most marked and special consideration."

The circumstances already mentioned (see p. 60) are here detailed, and some of his utterances on his deathbed quoted.

My father entirely concurred with the verdict thus pronounced; and the following year published a full account of Kaspar Hauser's story and of the fraud practised upon him. "I suppose," he used to say, "that I am the only man in the world that ever wrote a book to prove himself in the wrong"; yet he summed up his experiences with these generous words : "It cannot be denied, and I must myself confess, that Kaspar Hauser's statements were not to be trusted ; that he invented and misrepresented much ; and that in several instances, if not in his whole story, he deceived us ; but it must always remain a question whether he should be called an impostor in the usual acceptation of the word, and I hope that in this respect the world will judge the unhappy foundling fairly.

" I have no reason to believe that he came to Nuremberg with the intention of playing the part that was afterwards, in some measure, suggested to him ; and which, to the wonder of the world and the conviction of many very competent judges, he enacted with such extreme skill."

I wish I could here conclude the story of Kaspar Hauser. But the public interest, revived by his tragic and sensational end, would not suffer him to rest in his grave. Two rather scurrilous pamphlets, one reflecting on various crowned heads, and a lyric poem, appeared in 1835 ; but it was not till four years afterwards that the first attack upon my father (with the exception of one newspaper article, promptly refuted and contradicted) was given to the world. It was written, I am sorry to say, by a countrywoman, the English widow of a German officer—Countess Albersdorf, then an old woman

verging upon eighty. She had previously denounced three perfectly innocent men, two of
them as Kaspar's murderer ; and the Commissioners, before whom she appeared on the second
occasion, ungallantly describe her as "an extremely loquacious, foolish, and confused witness, bent upon repeating on hearsay all the
gossip of the town." In these two volumes
of *Revelations* she professed to have discovered
the secret of Kaspar's parentage, with the true
reason of his imprisonment ; and further pro-
claimed that my father had, from the time of
his first appearance at Nuremberg, organised
and concerted all the intrigues against him. It
was a tissue of follies and absurdities,[1] yet some
of this farrago of nonsense is gravely quoted
twenty years afterwards by Professor Daumer in
his even more scandalous work. This came out
in 1859, four years after my father's death ; and
is again entitled *Revelations on Kaspar Hauser,
by his former Tutor.* Daumer goes far beyond
the Countess in his denunciation. According to
him, Kaspar was the heir of a great English
house, sent early in life to Hungary, and only
adopted by Lord Stanhope in order that he
might the more easily oblige some English
friends who were (probably on account of an in-

[1] See p. 101.

heritance) interested in Kaspar's disappearance by making away with him. Not only did he direct the young man's assassination, but he also poisoned President von Feuerbach,[1] and even threatened Daumer's own life. The Professor declares that in 1835, when walking in an unfrequented street at Nuremberg, he met an extremely sinister-looking individual, who, from the suspicious action of his right hand, evidently meant mischief; and that the evil intention he thus divined was only frustrated by the merest accident! As an instance of his reasoning, I may note that he believed the bag dropped in the Hofgarten was Kaspar's own, but had been previously stolen from him to avert suspicion from the murderer.

Another newspaper, the *Neue Frankfurter Zeitung*, took up the theme in 1868. Its article, chiefly compiled from Countess Albersdorf's book, is full of gross inaccuracies and still grosser abuse of the wicked English Earl who had plotted the murder of his adopted son. Thus it is that slander grows. What was at first only the hint of a hideous suspicion had now developed into an uncontroverted fact.

[1] So far from being, as was alleged, totally unexpected, the President's death had been for some time anticipated, as he had never recovered from his first paralytic stroke in June 1832. The second killed him.

Dr. Meyer's son now endeavoured to stem the rising tide of calumny and falsehood. His father, who had always intended to write on the subject of his former pupil, was dead, and the duty thus devolved upon him. In 1870 he asked and obtained permission from the Minister of State to publish extracts from the numerous documents concerning Kaspar Hauser that were preserved in the archives of Munich, Ansbach, and Nuremberg, comprising all the evidence, reports, and judicial proceedings connected with the case, together with some private letters. Had it been possible, this should have been done years before ; but these police records being under the seal of official secrecy, their publication would not have been permitted at an earlier date. Dr. Julius Meyer was thus enabled to give to the world the only perfectly authentic account of the so-called " Child of Europe " ; and it is from this book that my narrative has been almost entirely derived.

Professor Daumer, however, remained unconvinced. In 1873 he wrote another controversial pamphlet : *Kaspar Hauser, his character, his innocence, his sufferings, and his origin thoroughly discussed and established,* in which he accused Dr. Meyer of having kept back part of the evidence and garbled the remainder. It was quite

true that the official documents had not been
given *in extenso;* they would have filled ten or
twelve volumes ; and who, piteously asked Dr.
Meyer, would ever have published, much less
bought and read these? But that he had per-
formed his task of selection fairly and conscientiously and never once swerved from the exact
truth, two very eminent jurists, both of them
well acquainted with the archives, readily came
forward to testify.

Another decade had passed before the story
cropped up again, and Professor Daumer was by
that time dead. In 1883 an anonymous pamphlet was published at Ratisbon, entitled *Kaspar
Hauser : the history of his life and the proof of
his royal birth. From the papers, now first
given to the public, of a person of the highest
rank.* It professed to contain some " most remarkable revelations," both " from official
sources hitherto inaccessible," and " from the
private notes of a man thoroughly conversant
with the case, who had at his disposal materials
very difficult of access." From this it might
fairly be inferred that some fresh information
was forthcoming, but this new publication was
simply a compilation of others that had appeared
forty or fifty years before, viz. :

1. *Kaspar Hauser, or the Foundling, ro-*

*mantically pourtrayed by* . . . Stuttgart, 1834.

2. *Kaspar Hauser, the heir to the throne of Baden.* Paris (in reality Zürich), 1840 : the preface by N. E. Mesis (Nemesis, *i.e.* Sebastian Seiler).

3. *Kaspar Hauser, or the true revelation of the secret of his birth : the cause of his imprisonment : its duration: analysis and signification of the letter he brought to the Bavarian captain : detailed specification of the man who received Kaspar as a child and then brought him as a young man to Nuremberg : Hauser's position at Nuremberg until his attempted assassination : finally, Lord Stanhope's first appearance at this time at Nuremberg, and the contrivance and preparation of the intrigues in which he was afterwards engaged.* By W. C. Gr. v. A. (Countess Albersdorf). 2 volumes. Munich, 1839.

4. A French pamphlet, privately circulated at Paris in 1870, without a title, or the name either of the author or printer.

No. 1 was taken from a pamphlet published in the same year at Strasburg by one Garnier, a refugee from Baden, then resident in Alsace, and entitled *Some contributions to the history of Kaspar Hauser, with a dramatic preface.* This

man was arrested at Baden seventeen years afterwards, and during his imprisonment deposed on
oath that this was a composition of his own, con-
cocted from common report and current rumours,
which he had published to revenge himself on
the Government that had proscribed him ; one
Engesser, to whom he bore a grudge, being
denounced as incriminated.

Of No. 2, Professor Daumer, the sworn
champion of Kaspar Hauser, says, " It breathes
throughout bitter enmity against princes and
priests. It is full of inaccuracies ; it is written
in the style of a novel or romance, and contains
one fantastic episode, which, from internal
evidence, is unmistakably a fiction. Who can
credit such things, without historical proof or
foundation, or indeed authority of any kind, on
merely anonymous testimony ? " Before it was
given to the public, this precious production,
with the promise of inviolable secrecy in the
future, had been three times offered to the Baden
Government ; first, for 1700 florins, next, for
1500 florins, and finally for 24 louis, and on
each occasion refused.

No. 3. Countess Albersdorf's two volumes
I have already described (p. 67). I may add
that she herself owns to a strong *animus* against
my father. It appears that she had twice asked

for an interview with him, and he had twice
excused himself from receiving her. She was
very indignant, and declared, " He will be sorry
some day that he would not see me."

No. 4 had of course a very limited circulation,
and Dr. Meyer had considerable difficulty in
procuring a copy. He thought he discerned in
it traces of the same hand that had been
employed on the new pamphlet.

The better to compare them, he printed in
1883 parallel passages from Nos. 1, 2, and 3,
and this last publication, which satisfactorily
establish their identity.

All recount, in great detail, a secret sitting of
the Council of State of Baden, held under the
presidency of Herr von Burniz, on the death of
the Grand-Duke Louis, with whom the elder
line of the House of Zaehringen expired, on
March 30, 1830. On this occasion Major von
Hennenhofer and other witnesses testified that
his nephew, their rightful sovereign, had been
set aside for reasons of State, and was then living
at Nuremberg, under the name of Kaspar
Hauser. The Grand-Duke Leopold, who
was present, with some difficulty prevailed
upon them to ignore his nephew's claim, and
name him as the next in succession to the
throne.

These so-called revelations profess to be extracts from the MS. memoirs of Major von Hennenhofer, which he valued so highly that he slept with them under his pillow, and had left instructions that they were to be given to the world at the end of the present century. These he had given to a former lawyer's clerk, named Seiler, to be copied, and Seiler, being dissatisfied with his remuneration, carried off his copy to Zürich, where he had it printed, and intended to publish it. But, before he could do so, the secret was betrayed to the Baden representative, Freiherr von Rüdt, who, in the name of his Government, demanded from the Swiss authorities the suppression of the entire edition, and the banishment of Seiler, who was, however, to receive payment.

This is a fabrication from beginning to end. Major von Hennenhofer, who was singled out for incrimination, was a Court favourite who had risen from the ranks, and as such, an exceedingly unpopular (and I believe deservedly unpopular) man. He was a voluminous writer; but no memoirs of any sort were found among his papers (now preserved in the archives of Karlsruhe), and all those acquainted with his style have pronounced Seiler's " Extracts " to be very clumsy forgeries. He himself, to his dying day, expressed the liveliest indignation at being suspected of complicity in such a conspiracy.[1]

Of the story itself, it need only be said that no Council of State existed in Baden at that date. It was only instituted thirty-three years afterwards, in 1863. The republication in 1883 of this and other allegations against the reigning House of Baden, was all the more unpardonable, as they had been refuted and exposed eight years before by Dr. Mittelstädt, in his *Kaspar Hauser and his Baden Princedom*. Heidelberg, 1875.

The accusations against my father were, if possible, even more extravagant and envenomed than those that had gone before. Not only had he been the accomplice of Countess Hochberg and Major von Hennenhofer, who had been employed to kidnap the Crown Prince of Baden, but he was himself " the soul of the conspiracy, the instigator and ringleader " of all the plots hatched against the unfortunate Hauser. He had been concerned in the attempted murder at Nuremberg. He had travelled to Ansbach with Hennenhofer in December 1833 for the purpose of finally despatching his victim, and " either with his own dagger, or that of a hired assassin,

---

[1] " The accusations and insinuations in all these pamphlets," he writes to one of his friends, " embitter my life."

inflicted the mortal wound. On them, and on those whose orders they obeyed, rests the burden of this crime, and the guilt of innocent blood."

Next came the turn of Dr. Meyer. " On him rested the grave suspicion of having delivered up to Lord Stanhope, Kaspar Hauser's journal " : this mysterious and unseen journal (see p. 61), which he fully believed had never been written. He was the servile "creature," the paid tool of the English Earl, initiated in all the evil secrets of his machinations, and had pocketed such heavy bribes, that from a poor man he had grown to be a rich one. Colonel Hickel, again, was another salaried conspirator, who had purposely absented himself from Ansbach on the day of Kaspar's assassination, in order to delay and hamper the judicial investigation it was his duty to conduct.

All this fury of vituperation was, it should be observed, levelled against men from whom no rejoinder was to be apprehended, as they had long since passed into the " eternal silence " of the grave. But Dr. Meyer's sons were not disposed to allow such vile imputations on their father's memory to pass unchallenged. They brought an action for libel against the publishers of these wicked slanders, and applied to me to join in the prosecution on my own father's behalf. My brother being dead, I now remained his nearest representative. But I refused to notice so foul a charge. I felt that, in stooping to answer it, I should be insulting, rather than vindicating his memory. I replied that if any people could be found to believe that he, or any English gentleman, had either himself used the dagger of an assassin, or employed that of a hired bravo, they must have altogether lost their understandings, and I did not see how the verdict of any tribunal could remedy their condition.

The cause was tried in April 1883, at Ratisbon, where the pamphlet had been published. No attempt was made to defend it, or uphold the libels it contained; the publisher only pleaded that he had acted in ignorance of the truth, and not from wilful malice. But he was sentenced to pay a fine of 100 florins, with costs, and ordered to destroy all the copies of the obnoxious publication that remained on his hands.

Some part of my father's correspondence with Dr. Meyer, and the last letter he wrote to Kaspar himself, dated Vienna, December 17, 1833, were read in court, to show the warm interest he had taken in his pupil's welfare, his thoughtful care,

and unwearied kindness.   His name was never
mentioned except with respect and commenda-
tion, and a due appreciation of his noble and
upright character.   One eminent jurist who gave
evidence, President Schmausz, declared that
" any one that studied the case must be lost in
amazement at the raving lunacy that could make
Lord Stanhope out a murderer." [1]

It might have been hoped that the Hauser
legend was now finally disposed of ; but this
was very far from being the case.   Scarcely four
years had elapsed before it cropped up again :
this time in a refutation of the story, entitled
*Kaspar Hauser : Eine neugeschichtliche Legende,
von Antonius von der Linde.*   But this publication scarcely met with the success it merited, for
we are told that " the historian Gregorovius "
(whoever he may be) only became " morally
certain " that Kaspar Hauser was Stéphanie's
son after reading Von der Linde's book.

Then in March 1892 a more ambitious title,
*Des Räthsels Lösung* (The Solution of the
Riddle), by Baron Alexander von Artin, held
out the prospect of something better than moral

---

[1] As I have a prejudice (evidently not shared by some
writers I might name) in favour of evidence taken on oath,
I have transcribed that part of the President's evidence
which bears out my own statements. (See p. 104.)

certainties. It contained two documents that were to set the matter at rest for ever, bequeathed by the Minister von Berstett to a prince whose name is not given, with the stipulation that they were not to be made public for fifty-five years after his death. This period had now elapsed.

One was the following letter in facsimile, purporting to be written by the Grand-Duke Louis, and dated June 5, 1828 :

"To my Government.

"In Nuremberg last month total failure. Take measures that this event does not disturb the peace of my Grand Duchy. Accept on my part the assurance of my continued interest in your welfare.—I remain, your well-affectioned

"LUDWIG."

This seems a remarkable circular for a sovereign, engaged in a nefarious conspiracy, to address to his Cabinet : and, to heighten its dramatic effect, it was delivered at midnight! I need scarcely add that it is entirely discredited in Germany. "A comparison made by experts of the handwriting and phraseology of this document with those of a great number of Cabinet papers of the reign of this Grand-Duke, plainly shows—independently of the contradictions in its arrangement and wording—that we have here to do with a clumsy forgery.

Besides other errors, the beginning and end is entirely different from that of similar official circulars. The address and superscription are in direct contradiction to the usual form. In particular, the Minister von Berstett (the whole of whose correspondence was made over by his widow to the Ministry of Foreign Affairs) never appears to have been so addressed."—*Karlsruher Zeitung*, March 11, 1892. "The only novelty contained in this publication is the reproduction in facsimile of a Cabinet circular respecting events said to have occurred at Nuremberg in 1828, probably to form the basis of future fables and suspicions. Several papers have already thrown doubts on its genuineness, and in fact a closer examination reveals unmistakable signs of forgery: a seal where no seal is ever placed; a superscription and address quite contrary to usage; four lines in a different handwriting from the rest; single words either displaced, or with a blank space left around them; a date fourteen years anterior to that of the water-mark of the paper, and so strangely written as to suggest its having been tampered with! A publication that, either wilfully or erroneously, makes use of methods such as these, cannot deserve any kind of notice."— *Badische Landeszeitung*, March 9, 1892.

The other document is Von Berstett's dying confession to the anonymous prince, which does not tell us much.    He avers that, though as long as he can remember, "the air was full of whispered suggestions that the first-born prince was still alive," he only became aware of it after the accession of the Grand-Duke Louis: and, hearing that the prince was "crippled and ruined in mind and body," he thought it best for the welfare of the State to keep the matter to himself.    "Also, I feared that if the truth were revealed, the unhappy Grand-Duchess Stéphanie would go mad.    Major Hennenhofer, whom I may well call my evil genius, knows more about this matter than I do.    After Leopold's accession, I found in his orders a good excuse for resigning my post."

The rest of the book is simply a reprint of the obnoxious publication prosecuted and condemned at Ratisbon in 1883, of which I have already spoken (see p. 70).    It is thus described by the judge who there pronounced the verdict :

"This work is shown to be compiled from former, partly anonymous, publications concerning Kaspar Hauser, which are, from internal evidence, utterly unworthy of belief, and accumulates falsehood upon falsehood, and suspicion upon suspicion—and these of the

G

worst kind ; as is likewise apparent in the
charges brought against Lord Stanhope, which
are well known to be utterly without foundation
in fact."

Not only is the prince who receives Von
Berstett's death-bed confession anonymous, but
the name given by the author is a pseudonym.
" Baron Alexander von Artin " is simply non-
existent.    No noble family of that name is to be
met with in Germany.    The author is supposed
to be a certain Von Ehrensberg, a native of
Baden, and once a captain in the Prussian service,
which he left, as is said, not entirely of his own
accord.    He then lived for some time at Zürich,
but, falling under the suspicion of being an in-
former,[1] was sent out of the country.    A work of
his on the Guelph Fund had been previously
published by the same firm at Zürich.

Some months after this, I am ashamed to
say that an English writer and a London firm
ventured to publish to the astounded world that
my father had been in the pay of the Grand-
Duke of Baden, and was the murderer of Kaspar
Hauser !    The various scurrilous and discredited
publications which I have described, hitherto un-
noticed in England, had been brought together

---

[1] The literal translation is *agent provocateur*, but I do
not know how to render this in English.

and translated to form " an interesting page of history," entitled *The Story of Kaspar Hauser, from authentic (i.e.* anonymous) *Records.* In my great indignation I would have welcomed the weapon of defence that I had rejected in Germany ; but I found that the law of England did not place it in my hands. The time that had since elapsed had relegated these ancient scandals, far beyond the reach of attack, into the neutral ground of History. History ! I might exclaim with Madame Roland, " what crimes are committed in thy name ! " I can imagine some future Macaulay, engaged in sifting the ashes of the lower strata of our literature, suddenly lighting upon this ghastly story, and pouring forth his indignation in a torrent of scathing eloquence : " What a state of society does this not reveal ! Here we have a lady — a lady doubtless of high social standing, perfectly conversant with the manners and customs of the nobility — openly accusing a nobleman of ancient and honourable lineage of being the hired bravo of the Grand-Duke of Baden ! True, she gives no proofs in support of her statement, but it is evident that the fact was even then—thirty-seven years after the Earl's death—so notorious as to need none. Her name—probably already familiar

to the literary world — was alone a sufficient
guarantee ; for no contradiction has ever been
attempted.    And  this  is  in  the  nineteenth
century !  in  the  reign  of  the  good  Queen
Victoria !   What must we think of the corruption and degradation of a time in which such
monstrous crimes passed unheeded ?   How is it
that we do not hear of this Earl's being brought
to justice, or at least expelled from the House
of Lords ?   Where is the boasted respectability
of our ancestors ?   We find this assassin—to
their shame be it spoken—taking part in the
debates  as  a  peer  of  parliament, addressing
crowded and enthusiastic public meetings, and
receiving addresses and testimonials in recognition of his services.   Then, what an indictment
is here against the Bible and missionary societies
that employed this caitiff as their *colporteur !*
Is it by hands such as these that Christianity is
to be disseminated ?   Yet, incredible as it may
appear, this polluted traffic was his principal
means of subsistence ; it was on this petty and
precarious pittance that his wife and family had
for years to struggle on ; and his abject poverty
might be pleaded as the sole excuse for his
being, as is stated, open to any bribe.   But we,
in this superior and more virtuous age, may
dismiss such paltry subterfuges with the scorn

they deserve, and rejoice that our standard of morality is not that of the disgraced and debased nineteenth century. All the more honour to the noble-minded woman who, ignoring any risk to her own character, boldly lifted the veil that had so long shrouded this hideous mystery, and earned the respect and gratitude of posterity, if not of her contemporaries!"

Here the author finds that he has missed one very telling point.

"But I must not be unjust. I must not leave untold the one striking incident that redeems the criminal apathy of the age. One English nobleman—and one only—was found honest enough to speak out. His voice alone is raised in the universal silence, and he, at least, does not shrink from proclaiming the truth. Lord Daniel Alban Durteal" (I have copied this nobleman's remarkable name with the most careful solicitude), "advocate of the Royal Court in London, said to . . ." (the writer of an anonymous letter): "'I am firmly convinced that Kaspar Hauser was murdered. It was all done by bribery. Stanhope has no money, and lives by this affair.'

"We know nothing of Lord Daniel Alban Durteal. His name has not been handed down to us in the pages of history. But it should be ever gratefully enshrined in the memory of his countrymen, and take its place beside that of the noble lady who so courageously bore witness to the truth with her pen. May we not please ourselves with the fancy that they were not altogether strangers to each other? that she may have been connected either by birth or marriage with the noble family of which he was the representative? or even, at one period of her life, herself borne the honoured name of Alban Durteal? Between their hearts, at least, there was true affinity."

I feel I am far from having done justice to the stirring passages that will delight our descendants in the future. But even this little attempt may serve to show how poor a figure the truth must cut by their side. How tame, flat, and altogether unsatisfying it must appear! Was it for this, men may well ask, that our best feelings were laid under contribution? Is it fair? Should so much good sympathy and honest indignation be utterly wasted and thrown away? Disappointment is not the word for it. Vexation would be a truer one.

And yet, with all this, there can be no question as to the result. It is not the highly wrought romance, but the plain and simple truth, that eventually wins the day. Not for a single moment have I faltered in this faith, or felt a misgiving as to the verdict I have to expect. I accept it before it is pronounced. One who bears the proud name of Englishwoman should be the last to doubt the good sense and right feeling of her countrymen ; and it is with the most perfect confidence that I leave my father's honour in their hands.

In his own words (written to Dr. Meyer on July 24, 1834) : "Truth is great and victorious, and much as we may now be maligned, through ignorance and prejudice, I have the conviction that in this, as in all other matters, it must in the end prove the conqueror."

# APPENDIX

# APPENDIX

EVIDENCE of the master shoemaker, George Leonard Weichmann, resident in the Unschlittsplatz in Nuremberg, taken on oath before the examining magistrate, November 4, 1829.

*Q.* What do you know in respect to Kaspar Hauser's first appearance in the year 1828 ?

*A.* I was standing at my house door on Easter Monday, when a young lad, the same shown to me before the magistrates under the name of Kaspar Hauser, came trudging down the Bärleinhuter hill. While still at some distance from me, he began to call out, " Hi, lad ! " and, as he came nearer, pronounced with tolerable distinctness the words, " Neue Thor Strasse ? " (New Gate Street). I supposed the lad wanted to go to some one in the Neue Thor Strasse, and offered to show him the way. I then went with Hauser over the Max Bridge towards the Neue Thor Strasse, when, not far from the bridge, he put his hand into the pocket of his jacket, and drew out a large sealed letter. He gave me the letter, and I read the address to the " Herr Rittmeister (Captain) of

the 4th Squadron." As I could give him no information respecting this gentleman, I said, "It will be
best for us to go to the guard-house at the Neue
Thor" (New Gate); and Hauser repeated, "Guard-
house—guard-house—Neue Thor no doubt just built?"
I explained to him that the Neue Thor was by no
means recently built, but only bore the name; and,
meanwhile, we were slowly approaching it. On the
way I asked Hauser where he came from. He said,
"Ratisbon"; and to my next question, whether he
had ever been here before, he replied, "No, it's the
first time." But when I went on to inquire what
news there was at Ratisbon, and what they said there
as to peace or war, Hauser indeed repeated my words,
"War — war"; but I soon perceived he had no idea
what war meant, and had not understood my question.
When we got to the Gate, the Police Examiner
called out, "Have you got a Wanderbuch?" (travelling journeyman's book, serving as a passport), but
omitted any further inquiries, as I explained that
Hauser had no Wanderbuch. Then I took him up
to the corporal and two other soldiers standing by.
Hauser took off his hat very respectfully, put it under
his arm, and showed the letter to the Herr Rittmeister.
The corporal took the letter, and the Examiner, pointing to the Gate, called out "Go straight in," and
when I saw that Kaspar went as directed, I went my
own way, not seeing—far less being able to tell—how
he reached the Rittmeister's house.

   *2.* How was Kaspar Hauser dressed on this, his
first appearance?

   (Witness here described and identified the clothes.)

*2*. Doubts have been expressed as to whether Kaspar Hauser really used the words you reported—"Ratisbon, Neue Thor no doubt just built." Have you a distinct remembrance of them?

*A*. I distinctly remember hearing Kaspar Hauser pronounce the words as I reported them.

Weichmann was again examined in May 1834, and recapitulated his former evidence, adding the following details:—

I was standing talking to the shoemaker, Jacob Beck, and we had been chatting together about ten minutes when I saw a young stranger, afterwards named Kaspar Hauser, come down the tolerably steep Bärleinhuter hill at a good pace. . . . He was not bent down, as has been asserted, but walked like any one else; and as long as he was with me, stood firm on his feet and did not stagger. But he was evidently jaded, and rather dusty, as 'if he had just walked a long way. Beck said to me it would be well if I showed him the Neue Thor Strasse, as in any case I was going that way. This I accordingly did. Kaspar Hauser kept step with me, and it would have been folly to think of leading him. . . . About ten days after this Kaspar Hauser was brought before the Town Council, that I might identify him. But he would not recognise me, and when I asked him if he did not remember me, replied, "No, no"; and this he said in a tone that might have led one to suppose him to be dazed. While the questions and answers recorded in the minutes were being read out, I kept my eyes fixed on his face, and when he observed I was watching him, he cried impatiently, "What makes

you stare at me so?" . . . He was very tolerably
dressed; I have already described his clothes (before
the magistrates). His dress, appearance, and general
demeanour was that of a stable boy.

EVIDENCE of the shoemaker, Jacob Beck of Nuremberg, taken on oath before the examining magistrate, May 5, 1834.

On the afternoon of the day that Kaspar Hauser
first came to Nuremberg, I was standing with the
shoemaker Weichmann at the corner of the Unschlittsplatz and the middle Kreuzgasse, when we
saw Kaspar coming down the Bärleinhuter hill with
a firm step. He was really a droll figure, for he wore
very wide trousers, a short jacket, and on his head a
low-crowned hat, which looked very comical. I took
him for a journeyman tailor just arrived. As he came
nearer, he cried with a distinct but rather broken
voice, "Where's Neue Thor Strasse?" As I knew
Weichmann was going in that direction, I told him
he ought to take the stranger with him; and so he
did. I myself went another way. Afterwards I heard
from Weichmann that he had mentioned before the
Town Council our being together when Kaspar came
down the Bärleinhuter hill. This is all I know of
Kaspar Hauser. If I could have guessed that this
Kaspar Hauser was such an interesting person, I
would certainly have gone with him to the Neue Thor
Strasse; but as it was he looked to me a very ordinary
sort of fellow.

EVIDENCE of Johann Matthew Merk, servant of the Rittmeister von Wessenig, taken on oath before the examining magistrate, December 20, 1829.

On that Easter Monday my master and all his household were absent, and I left alone in the house, when, about seven o'clock in the evening, the door bell rang. I went from the stable to open the front door, and found there the same young man whom I often saw afterwards under the name of Kaspar Hauser. He wore a gray jacket, and trousers of the same, with a round hat, and showed me a letter he held in his hand, saying that he "wanted to be a trooper, as his father was," and that he had been "directed to come here to this house." I asked him where he came from, to whom the letter was addressed, etc., but could get nothing out of him except, "I don't know." Young Hauser was very tired : so much so that he reeled as he walked, and pointed to his feet to show that they hurt him ; and as I thought, because he had a letter for the Herr Rittmeister, that I was bound to let him stay, I took him to the stable, where he lay down on the straw. He took bread and water greedily, but turned with disgust from the meat and beer offered him. Towards eight o'clock the Herr Rittmeister came home. I do not remember being present when he found Hauser in the stable ; I only know that Hauser was afterwards got rid of, and that he was scarcely able to walk.

2. Who had rung the bell when you opened the house door to admit Kaspar Hauser ?

*A.* I cannot speak of my own knowledge, but as I found Kaspar Hauser standing at the door quite alone, I conclude it must have been him.

## RE-EXAMINATION of Merk on May 5, 1834.

Kaspar Hauser looked quite healthy, but his feet were swollen, and he was very dusty, as if he had just come in from a long journey. He seemed to understand all that was said well enough, but he did not speak very intelligibly, but rather unconnectedly, and with evident difficulty. We had a long chat. He told me he did not know where he came from, and began to cry about it; then he distinctly said that he had been forced to travel day and night; that he had been carried when he could no longer walk: that he had learnt to read and write; and that he had to cross the frontier every day to go to school. When I showed him the horses, he said, quite distinctly, "There were five like that where I came from." This is all I know of Kaspar Hauser.

*Q.* Did you satisfy yourself that he really could read and write?

*A.* I cannot affirm it on oath: I don't quite remember.

*Q.* It is stated that you sat together on a stone bench, and that he wrote his name in pencil: is that true?

*A.* Yes, I believe I saw Kaspar Hauser write, but I cannot swear to it.

EVIDENCE of Johann Hacker, coachman of Rittmeister von Wessenig, taken on oath before the examining magistrate, November 2, 1829.

Kaspar Hauser, on arriving at Nuremberg, and coming to the house of Rittmeister von Wessenig, whom I served as coachman, took great delight in the horses : he was very sorry to part from them, and kept on patting them. When he first came, the Herr Rittmeister was not at home, but was attending the consecration of the church at Erlangen. I had to drive him there : and when we came back in the evening, Kaspar Hauser was lying asleep on the straw, curled up, and as it were rolled together, for he had drawn his legs close up to his body.

EVIDENCE of the Rittmeister of the 4th Squadron of the 6th Bavarian Regiment of Cavalry, Friedrich von Wessenig, taken on oath before the examining magistrate, November 2, 1829.

On the evening of that Easter Monday, when I returned from a drive with the Commissioner of Police, Von Scheurl, and Lieutenant von Hugenpoët, I was told that a stranger bringing a letter was waiting for me, lying on the straw in the stable : that they could not make him out : that they offered him meat and beer, which he would not touch : and that he had taken nothing but bread and water. I went myself to the stable, accompanied by the Commissioner and the Lieutenant, and found a young peasant asleep on the straw. I had him awakened : and when he saw me,

H

he came up to me, smiling, said, " I want to be such a one " : took hold of my *porte-épée*, and began playing with it. I asked him his name ; he replied that his foster-father had desired him to say only " I don't know, your Honour " ; then he took off his hat, adding, " My foster-father said I was always to take off my hat and say your Honour," and made me a bow. Meanwhile my servant delivered the letter he had brought, and I read it through. Its tone of importunity and insistence provoked me ; and I therefore handed it to the Police Commissioner who was present, asking him to take charge of the boy. This he at once agreed to do : and my servant led him to the Police Court, as the lad was not well able to walk alone, being tired and footsore. In other respects he looked healthy, and well-fed : the peasant's dress he wore seemed clean and quite new : and he had with him a Catholic prayer-book and a cotton handkerchief : there was a name written in the prayer-book, but it was so effaced that it could not be made out. When I had him taken away, he was very loath to leave the stable, complained of pain in his feet, and seemed greatly pleased with the horses, repeating " Ross " (horse). During the short time I had the opportunity of observing him while he was in my house, I judged him to be entirely uneducated and so to speak in a state of Nature, and the possibility of any deception on his part was not to be thought of.

EVIDENCE of the police-corporal Christopher Wüst,
sworn on his official duty, May 5, 1834.

On the day that Kaspar Hauser first arrived, he was
brought to our guard-room, where I was on duty. I
was about three hours with Kaspar in this room. He
was very loutish-looking, with a healthy complexion,
and of very stout build. He certainly appeared neither
pale nor delicate, and I should have said that, instead
of living in confinement, he had been a great deal in
the open air, but he showed a considerable amount of
fatigue. When light was brought in, he did not
shrink from it, nor did his eyes seem to be sensitive to
light. I wrote down directions on a piece of paper
that he was to sign his name, with the name of the
place he came from; then I gave him a pen ready
dipped in ink, and he came quite close to the light
without the slightest apparent discomfort. He held
the pen properly, just like other people, and wrote his
name quite legibly, though far from well. The only
thing that struck me while he was writing was that
his hand shook a little. He did not write down what
place he came from. I showed him my paper again,
desiring him to tell me the name of this place, and
he answered, without hesitation and in a distinct voice,
" I dare not say." I then asked why he dared not tell,
and he replied, clearly and decidedly as before, " Because
I don't know." This was the only answer he would
give to all the other questions that I put to him, so
that I had but little conversation with him.

EVIDENCE of the police-soldier Jean Jaques Lemarier,
   sworn on his official duty, May 5, 1834.

On the first day that Kaspar Hauser came to
Nuremberg, he was brought into our guard-room,
where I was, and I was then with him for about two
hours.   He held himself quite upright, and walked up
and down the room with short steps, not appearing
fatigued—at least he did not complain of fatigue : and
during the two hours he was in the guard-room never
asked to sit down.

Compare these matter-of-fact statements with
Professor Feuerbach's sensational account of Kaspar
Hauser on his first arrival at Nuremberg.

"A tradesman, dwelling in the so-called Unschlittsplatz in Nuremberg, was loitering before his
door, about to go from thence to the so-called Neue
Thor, when, on turning round, he perceived, not far
from him, a young man, dressed as a peasant, who was
standing in a most unusual attitude ; and—as if intoxicated—was trying to move forward without holding
himself upright, or being able to direct his steps.
The tradesman went up to this stranger, who held
out to him a letter addressed to the Rittmeister of the
4th Squadron of the Schmolische Regiment.   As the
Rittmeister lived near the Neue Thor, the tradesman
conducted the stranger thither." *Beispiel eines Ver-*
*brechens am Seelenleben des Menschens* (Instance of
a Crime against a Human Soul) : pp. 1, 2.

"Kaspar Hauser showed such an utter deficiency of
words and ideas, such perfect ignorance of the com-

monest things and appearances of Nature, such horror
of all the customs, conveniences, and necessities of
civilised life, and with all this, such extraordinary
peculiarities in his social, mental, and physical disposi-
tion, that one might have felt one's self driven to the
alternative of believing him to be the citizen of another planet, transferred by some miracle to our own :
or else for the man described by Plato, who was born
and grew up under the earth, and only emerged to the
light of day when he had attained the age of manhood."
*Ibid.*, pp. 20, 21.


EVIDENCE of Andreas Hiltel, warder of the Tower
    Prison in the Castle of Nuremberg, November
    1829.

On his first arrival, Kaspar Hauser's feet were, not
indeed sore, but much swollen, as his boots were very
tight. Moreover, it should be noted, that to judge
from his feet, it may be safely assumed that he had
been more in the habit of walking barefoot than in
boots. During the time he was in my charge he at
first sat always on a bench, and only later on used a
chair. At the beginning he sat rather bent down ; and
neither on the bench nor on the ground did he ever
stretch out his legs, but tucked them under him, like a
tailor. When he was asleep, too, he lay curled up,
and drew up his legs.

## Countess Albersdorf.

As a specimen of Countess Albersdorf's writings, I have here given a literal translation of two extracts from this book.

" Some time after this I had a vision, in which Hauser appeared to me.  I was at Ansbach, and went to the cemetery, through the gate of which two men were passing out, engaged in a heated colloquy.  I let them pass, and entered the cemetery.  There I saw Kaspar, with his arms stretched out, hurrying after these gentlemen, as if he wished to detain them ; but he could not pass the gate, and was obliged to stop. Struck by this apparition, I asked, 'For God's sake, Kaspar ! I thought you were dead ?' on which he sighed deeply, and pointed with his right hand to the bleeding wound, from which the blood was dripping down even to his feet.  'Then it is true !' I said ; 'they say you took your own life ; tell me, Kaspar, is that true ?'  Whereupon he gazed piteously up to Heaven, and shook his head.  On this I said, 'Kaspar, I am convinced of your innocence, and swear to you in the name of God that I will defend your honour as far as lies in my power' ; at this assurance his countenance brightened ; he folded his hands together three times in supplication, and vanished.  Since then I have no peace " . . .

Then followed a second vision :

" I was transported into an Eden-like country, of which no pen can describe the beauty.  I beheld an illimitable meadow, covered with the loveliest and most balsam-breathing flowers. While I was still gazing on all these marvels, Hauser came across the meadow towards me, greeted me, and gave me his hand. His countenance was transfigured, and his dress as magnificent as any worn by a courtier on a gala night at court; on his breast were the decorations of two great Orders. I cried in surprise, 'Hauser, what great change has come over you?' Pointing to the Orders on his breast, he answered, 'This is what I should have attained to, had I lived.' 'Oh, forget all that!' I said; 'you are sufficiently recompensed for all your sorrows in the world, now that you are translated into this heavenly paradise.' He now took me by the hand and led me, he still walking in the meadow, and I on the sand-strewn path, from the eminence into a most beautiful valley, through which flowed a crystal-clear river; here he turned, took my other hand, and led me back by the same way to a place strewn with such priceless and dazzling precious stones that my eyes were quite blinded, and I cried in delight, 'This is no earthly treasure!' And while I was still rapt in the contemplation of this splendour and beauty, he said warningly, 'Be steadfast, and not irresolute, and keep your promise.' As I turned to look at him he had vanished. My eyes sought him, and found him walking towards a hill. 'That is the way to Ansbach!' I cried; 'he goes to his grave, to visit his bones.' At this outcry all disappeared."

I confess myself much "fetched" by the idea that men may receive in paradise the decorations they have failed to obtain on earth.

## TRIAL FOR LIBEL.

The case was tried on April 16, 1883, in the Schaffen Court at Ratisbon, before Oberlandgerichts rath[1] von Ammon.

The plaintiff, Dr. Julius Meyer, was represented by the advocate Hänle.

The defendant, Von Coppenrath (the publisher), by the advocate Adlmann.

The defence set up was that Von Coppenrath had accepted the book, in good faith, from a friend and correspondent of Professor Daumer's, who had inspired him with the most perfect confidence. No vindication was even attempted; for any intention of upholding the truth of the statements it contained was formally and expressly disclaimed; and Von Coppenrath declared he had never seen Dr. Meyer's book till a fortnight before the trial.

The verdict I have already given.

## EXAMINATION of President Karl Schmausz of Nuremberg.

*Hänle.* Are you acquainted with the Acts[2] now preserved in the archives of Ansbach, as well as those at Nuremberg, relating to the violent death of the foundling Kaspar Hauser?

*Schmausz.* Yes, I read them—if not word for word

---

[1] In mercy to the English reader, I have omitted some of this gentleman's titles.

[2] Official documents are so called in Germany.

—in the year 1868 or 1869; they were then kept in the Court Registry Office, and, as I had often talked over the case with the late Dr. Meyer, I took an interest in it: all the more that, being a native of Ansbach, I had heard a great deal about it already.

*Hänle.* Did these Acts give you the impression that the investigation had been careless, superficial, or incomplete?

*Schmausz.* No investigation was ever conducted with greater care than this. I would only observe that, as regards the Nuremberg Acts, they are not free from bias. The object then intended and kept in view was to prove that Kaspar Hauser was of noble origin; and it was from this standpoint that the inquiry was carried on.

*Hänle.* Do Dr. Julius Meyer's *Authentic Communications respecting Kaspar Hauser* (the book mentioned in p. 82) correspond with the contents of these Acts?

*Schmausz.* Yes, as far as my memory serves me. My decided impression is that they gave all the salient points of the case. I am quite positive that nothing really essential was left out. These *Authentic Communications* appeared in the year 1872, and led to great attacks on Dr. Meyer. He asked me to bear witness that they contained all the essential points of the case. I gave him this testimony, and my letter was afterwards reprinted in the *Allgemeine Zeitung*.

*Hänle.* Does it appear from these Acts that the late Dr. Meyer was suspected of knowledge or complicity in any crime committed against Kaspar Hauser?

*Schmausz.* As far as I know, there is no trace of this in the Acts; and I am convinced that in the year

1834, when the investigation as to murder was proceeding, there was no idea of any suspicion of the kind. As far as I remember, Dr. Meyer was then held to be an unimpeachable authority. He was of a frank and open character; a man of undoubted and unquestioned integrity and uprightness. No one in Ansbach suspected him of a base or criminal action. And he was one of the best-known persons there.

*Hänle.* Was the book published by his sons intended to remove any suspicion from their father at the cost of Kaspar Hauser?

*Schmausz.* I think not; the origin of this work will prove it.

It may have been in the summer of 1858 that I met the plaintiff's father at an evening party. The conversation turned on Kaspar Hauser, who has always been a "curiosity"; and Dr. Meyer was thus involuntarily led into telling me, and one or two other gentlemen present, a great deal about what had occurred during the two years that Kaspar lived in his house as his pupil.

I may say, that though till then I had formed no very definite opinion regarding Kaspar Hauser, Dr. Meyer, on that evening, in the course of a conversation that lasted for two hours, entirely convinced me of the correctness of his point of view. Since then, I have held the decided opinion that the popular version of Kaspar Hauser's life, especially as given by President von Feuerbach, is founded on a delusion; and that Kaspar Hauser, either at his first appearance or later on, inundated the world with lies and fictions about himself. Every one may be mistaken, Dr. Meyer as

well as myself, but I can say with perfect sincerity that
he entirely convinced me.   Then he told us he had
kept notes (at that time about twenty-five years old)
about Kaspar Hauser, and thought of publishing them.
I told him he was quite right, as the case had grown
into a sort of historical problem, and it would be a
good thing to have it cleared up.

The bookseller Seybold in Ansbach soon after
announced the forthcoming publication of a *Life of
Kaspar Hauser*, by Dr. Meyer.   But this project fell
through ; and meanwhile years rolled on.   Dr. Meyer
never published his book, and died in 1868.

Since then I have often spoken to his son about it,
and urged him to undertake it as a sort of legacy from
his father, and to clear up the story before the world.
But I can safely say that neither then, nor when
speaking to his father on the subject, had I the
slightest idea of any suspicion that this work was intended to avert.   Neither I nor any one else ever
thought of such a thing.

*The Judge.*  Did you think him capable of an action
similar to that imputed to him in Coppenrath's
publication ?

*Schmausz.*  Not in the remotest degree.

*Hänle.*  Did the Acts give you the impression that
Lord Stanhope was " the soul and motive-power of all
the plots against Kaspar Hauser " ?

*Schmausz.*  No impression of the kind.   The Acts
show the exact reverse, though they do not contain
much about him.   But when one studies the case, one
is lost in amazement at the raving lunacy that would
make Lord Stanhope out to be a murderer.   Lord

Stanhope was an Englishman, and, like all Englishmen,
came to Germany on the look-out for curiosities : and
just as such another Englishman might nowadays
walk into Pickert's curiosity-shop in Nuremberg,
Lord Stanhope went after Kaspar Hauser. That was
the probable reason of their being brought together.
As time went on—for Lord Stanhope was a noble-
hearted and benevolent man—he grew fond of him,
and enacted the part of a father towards him ; but ·
that he was a murderer is perfectly incredible.

*The Judge.* That is proved by the letter Kaspar
Hauser received from him on the day of his wound.

*Schmausz.* Yes : that letter was written by Stanhope
at Vienna, before his departure for Munich, to Kaspar
Hauser, then already wounded, at Ansbach, evidently
in the best possible intention ; and I cannot conceive
how any one could wander so far afield in the realms
of imagination as to describe Lord Stanhope as a
murderer.  It is a deplorable hallucination.

*The Judge.* It had been already stated in the Paris
pamphlet.

*Hänle.* And by the Albersdorf.

*The Judge.* Kaspar was not heir to a throne ?

*Schmausz.* I may be permitted to remark, that as
far as I remember, I never spoke about the Baden
Princedom to Dr. Meyer, and I do not think that I
mentioned it to his son in 1868 or 1869.  In point of
fact, there is not a single thread of evidence that
connects Ansbach with Karlsruhe.  Even supposing
that a prince of Baden had been set aside—an
assumption long since disproved by Mittelstädt—it
would not follow that a problematical individual who

turns up at Nuremberg eighteen years afterwards must be that prince.

*The Judge.* The family likeness would have shown it.

*Hänle.* I have studied this question a good deal, and if all the assertions that have been made are correct, the princes of the elder line of Zaehringen must all have been exactly alike; for at one time Kaspar is so strikingly like one prince that he might be mistaken for him : then equally like another prince : and finally like a third.

*Schmausz.* Feuerbach also discovered in him a likeness to the Canon Guttenberg.

*Hänle* (quoting Feuerbach). " Hauser is, so to speak, a canon *en miniature.*"

Do you know whether, as stated in Coppenrath's publication, the experts examined before the Commission " gave incontrovertible testimony that the wound could not possibly have been self-inflicted " ?

*Schmausz.* As regards that, I only remember it is stated in the Acts, that, of the two experts, the first, Dr. Horlacher, held an unfavourable opinion of Kaspar's statement, and the second, Dr. Albert, a more favourable one. Otherwise I remember nothing of their report.

*Hänle.* One question more — Are you acquainted with Triesdorf, and is there a country house near there named Schloss Falkenhaus ? [1]

*Schmausz.* I know Triesdorf very well indeed. The house is called in the anonymous publication

---

[1] This is in allusion to another of the random statements contained in the book. The place of Kaspar Hauser's incarceration was discovered to be Falkenhaus, a shooting lodge secluded in the depths of a Royal forest, and far removed from all human habitation.

Falkenhaus by Triesdorf. That is an incorrect description. Triesdorf is a Royal park, about an hour and a half's drive in circuit, and enclosed by a brick wall. Within this are a number of dwelling-houses, forming a kind of village—little villas, public-houses, etc. In the midst of these stands Falkenhaus, no more isolated than the house we are in now, and surrounded by gardens and shrubberies.

*Hänle.* Was there a garrison at that time in the place?

*Schmausz.* I don't doubt that there was a garrison then, and am pretty sure there was once—from the year 1792—a Prussian garrison. During the thirty years over which my recollections extend, there has always been a garrison at Triesdorf. I have no doubt there was one previously, but I cannot speak of my own knowledge.

*Hänle.* Is Falkenhaus on the high road?

*Schmausz.* A broad carriage road passes through Triesdorf and leads to Weidenbach, only about a rifle-shot distant.

*The Judge.* Is the Unschlittsplatz in Nuremberg near the gate by which you enter in coming from Neumarkt?

*Schmausz.* No. From Neumarkt you enter by the Frauenthor. From there to the Unschlittsplatz there is a greater distance—perhaps a quarter of an hour's drive.

*The Judge.* It is supposed that Hauser came from Neumarkt. He spoke Low Bavarian.

*Hänle.* His first word was " Bua " (lad).

*Schmausz.* He never learnt that at Triesdorf, nor at Nuremberg either.

*Adlmann.* May I ask whether you read the Acts,

or merely looked them over ?    How far do they correspond with the *Authentic Communications ?*

*Schmausz.* I read them.    I am a practical "Kriminalist,"[1] and have been all my life engaged in reading Acts.    I wished to inform myself regarding this case, as I took an interest in it.    I naturally did not read these gigantic masses of evidence through from beginning to end, but I read every Act I considered of importance, and these *Communications* therefore contained nothing that was new to me.    Nor have I discovered in them either changes or omissions.    When the book first appeared, I said to Dr. Meyer, " I only wish you had published the Acts in full, word for word."    " But," Meyer objected, " who would then publish or buy the book ? "    I said at the time, if they are not published word for word, it will be alleged that something or other has been suppressed.

*Hänle.* They found an easier way than that, for the Acts are said to have disappeared at Vienna.

*Adlmann.* Have not the Acts, or some part of them, really disappeared ?

*Schmausz.* The magisterial Acts in Nuremberg have disappeared.    But it is perfectly clear, from Feuerbach's book, that these Acts militated *against* the view he took of Kaspar Hauser.    Feuerbach himself says they contain a number of anachronisms. Stanhope mentions a noteworthy expression of his regarding them.    Feuerbach once said to him, " Those Acts ought to be burned !    When one studies those Acts one begins to think that Kaspar Hauser was a liar ! "

---

[1] That is, versed in criminal law.

*Adlmann.* Are you aware that Dr. Heidenreich was the first doctor who examined Kaspar Hauser after he had received his first wound?

*Schmausz.* I only know it as a fact from having read it either in the Acts or the *Communications.*

*Adlmann.* And you are likewise aware that Dr. Heidenreich, who made this examination, held that the theory of suicide was inadmissible?

*Schmausz.* I have Heidenreich's finding here. It tells us that he, as well as Dr. Albert, held that opinion, but he expressly adds, and that in the plainest possible words—even Daumer's book admits this— that the possibility of a suicide could not be kept out of view.

Here follows a long account of the finding of a stiletto in the Hofgarten (see p. 57), by a forester named Pausch, etc.

THE END

*Printed by* R. & R. CLARK, *Edinburgh.*